KATIE ZHAO

RANDOM HOUSE 🏠 NEW YORK

Text copyright © 2022 by Katherine Zhao
Jacket art copyright © 2022 by Sher Rill Ng

All rights reserved. Published in the United States by
Random House Children's Books, a division of
Penguin Random House LLC, New York.

Random House and the colophon are registered trademarks of
Penguin Random House LLC.

Visit us on the Web! rhcbooks.com

Educators and librarians, for a variety of teaching tools, visit us at
RHTeachersLibrarians.com

Library of Congress Cataloging-in-Publication Data
Names: Zhao, Katie, author.
Title: Winnie Zeng unleashes a legend / Katie Zhao.
Description: First edition. | New York : Random House Children's Books, [2022] |
Summary: Armed with her fledgling powers, a magic cookbook, and the mentorship of
a talking rabbit, sixth grader Winnie Zeng must embrace her heritage and the powers of
her ancestors to save her town from an evil spirit of Chinese legend.
Identifiers: LCCN 2021017563 (print) | LCCN 2021017564 (ebook) |
ISBN 978-0-593-42657-9 (trade) | ISBN 978-0-593-42658-6 (lib. bdg.) |
ISBN 978-0-593-42659-3 (ebook)
Subjects: LCSH: Chinese American children—Juvenile fiction. |
Chinese American families—Juvenile fiction. | Magic—Juvenile fiction. | Spirits—
Juvenile fiction. | Sisters—Juvenile fiction. | Grandmothers—Juvenile fiction. |
Middle schools—Juvenile fiction. | Friendship—Juvenile fiction. | CYAC:
Chinese Americans—Fiction. | Magic—Fiction. | Spirits—Fiction. | Sisters—
Fiction. | Grandmothers—Fiction. | Middle schools—Fiction. | Schools—Fiction. |
Friendship—Fiction. | LCGFT: Paranormal fiction.
Classification: LCC PZ7.1.Z513 Wi 2022 (print) | LCC PZ7.1.Z513 (ebook) |
DDC 813.6 [Fic]—dc23

Printed in the United States of America
10 9 8 7 6 5 4 3 2 1
First Edition

Kitchen appliances and tools are not toys and should be used carefully.
The activities described on pages 274–276 require cooking and should be
performed under adult supervision and with an adult's permission.

For those who have ever felt powerless or invisible,
Winnie's tale of empowerment and joy is for you.

CHAPTER ONE

Middle school. Is there a scarier place on the planet? In books and movies, everything bad happens in middle school. Kids get bullied. Kids go through puberty. Teachers might turn into monsters or, worse, give out *real homework*.

Middle school has been ruining young lives for so long, there's an ancient Chinese proverb that goes, "Middle school is the worst three years of a person's life." Okay, I may have made that one up, but if you ask me, it should be a proverb. Maybe middle school wasn't so bad in ancient China.

Anyway, I planned to be as well equipped as possible to face down the beast known as middle school. I tried to buy a sword on eBay, but my parents stopped me and yelled about "buying dangerous weapons online," even after I explained that the only danger was in me attending middle school without proper equipment. That didn't go over very well, either.

As a result, I was forced to be resourceful. All summer before starting sixth grade at Groton Middle School, I studied movies, comic books, and anime to learn how to survive the upcoming school year. I practiced my roundhouse kicks in case an eighth-grade bully tried to shove me into a locker (something that was likely to happen daily, according to movies). Another common middle school occurrence, based on my reading of comic books and anime: kids discovering their hidden magic or superpowers and saving the world from evil adults. So I bought a pink cape and sparkly pink tights and memorized the *Sailor Moon* theme song. The chances were pretty slim, but just in case the Sailor Scouts came knocking on my door, asking me to join them in fighting evil by moonlight, I had to be prepared.

Then there was my real-life research on middle school, which came from my fourteen-year-old sister, Lisa. She'd just graduated from Groton Middle School and moved on to the only place more frightening than middle school: high school. Observing Lisa for the past three years had taught me exactly what *not* to do.

Still, all of my middle school readiness wasn't enough to prepare me for the scream that woke me up on the first day of school:

"WINNIE, GET OUT OF BED AND HELP ME MAKE BREAKFAST!"

My mother's shouting jerked me out of sleep. Groaning and rubbing my eyes, I rolled over to check my clock. It was only seven in the morning. Every other eleven-year-old on the planet was still fast asleep. Thanks to the nightmare I had last night, I'd barely slept a wink.

It was the same nightmare I'd had for almost two weeks

straight, ever since I lost first prize in the statewide piano competition by only half a point. In my nightmare, the judge, who bore a suspicious resemblance to my mother, handed me the first-place trophy. But as soon as I reached out a hand to grab it, the Mama-judge snatched it back and announced that she'd made an error, and first place actually went to a giant marshmallow. For coming in second, I received . . . a truckload of SAT prep books.

"What the heck? Why am I being *punished*?" I cried out.

"This is for your own good, Winnie." The Mama-judge opened the truck's back door, revealing towering piles of workbooks. I tried to run but found that my feet were frozen. A huge, wobbling stack of books fell out of the truck and landed right on top of—

"ARGHHH NOOOOOO!"

I'd woken up from the nightmare drenched in sweat at three a.m. Even though I was exhausted, it took me a whole hour to fall back asleep. I hadn't exactly been eager to see the conclusion of that nightmare.

In reality, I had lost the first-place trophy not to a giant marshmallow but to David Zuo, a.k.a. the single most annoying eleven-year-old in the whole country. Actually, make that the whole Western Hemisphere.

David attended my Sunday Chinese school, and we had the same piano teacher. As far back as I could remember, Mama was constantly comparing me with him. (*Did you see that David won another Chinese language contest? Did you hear that David got a perfect score on his piano test?*) And in my parents' eyes, David Zuo could do no wrong. Though, of course, they didn't know him like I did. They didn't know that sometimes he went out of his way to show me that he'd gotten a higher score on a Chinese test, the jerk. They didn't know that if you looked up *obnoxious* in the dictionary, you'd find his picture. It was up to me to prove to my parents that I could be just as good as—no, better than—David at anything and everything.

This was the second time in a row that I'd lost the piano competition to that turd David. It wasn't exactly a successful start to the new school year, but at least I had the whole rest of the year to work on it.

"Stop thinking about David," I ordered myself. Even though David had ruined part of my summer, at least there was no chance of him ruining middle school for me, too. He went to some smarty-pants private school in the next town over. I still reigned at the top of my grade, and I planned to keep it that way all throughout middle school.

"WINNIE! DON'T MAKE ME COME UP THERE!" Mama threatened.

"Coming!" I'd promised my mother yesterday that we'd wake up early and make breakfast together. And if there was one thing that could get me to leave my bed, it was the promise of food.

I grabbed the first-day-of-school outfit that I'd left hanging on my desk chair: a white sundress Mama had bought on sale at T.J. Maxx. Bounding down the stairs, I quickly combed through the tangles of my long black hair with a brush, which Mama had also picked up from the clearance rack at T.J. Maxx. (There was nothing my mother loved more than finding a good bargain at that store.) Then I styled it into my signature hairstyle, two long braided pigtails.

"What're we making?" I asked as I walked into the kitchen.

Mama wrapped her flower-printed apron around her waist and then handed me mine, which had a panda design. "Your favorite. Scallion pancakes."

At the thought of the savory dish, my mouth watered. Mama had already gotten out all the ingredients, so my job was to stir them together in a big mixing bowl.

By the time I'd finished and Mama had heated the pan, my older sister, Lisa, poked her head into the kitchen with a sleepy-looking expression. "Morning." She made a beeline for the box of Frosted Flakes on top of the refrigerator, which was pretty much all she ever ate for breakfast.

"Put that cereal away," Mama ordered, pointing at Lisa with her spatula. "We're having scallion pancakes for breakfast."

"But we have Chinese food, like, every meal of every day," Lisa whined.

"Well, we are Chinese people," Mama pointed out.

"That doesn't mean we can't eat *other* food."

I tried my best to tune them out. Mama and Lisa had this

argument almost daily. Ever since Lisa had started hanging out with the "popular" crowd back in middle school, she thought that Chinese food was uncool. *Popular* in middle school meant taking pride in mediocre grades and having parents who spoiled the heck out of you. Oh, and not eating good food, apparently.

"—and don't even bother trying to appeal to your father to let you eat that cereal junk," Mama was saying to Lisa. "He's already gone to the office for the day."

Baba was always at the office. If he could, he would probably sleep there. He worked as a lawyer, which meant he got to yell at people for a living and came home at really odd hours. One time I woke up at midnight because of a loud banging noise in the kitchen. I thought our house was being robbed, so I grabbed my tennis racket and ran downstairs. Before I could show off my sweet serve by aiming the ball at the "criminal," like I'd learned from the manga *The Prince of Tennis*, the "criminal" had flipped on the light and started yelling at me. Turned out Baba had been heating up leftovers for a late dinner, and he didn't appreciate nearly being beaned on the heinie with a tennis ball.

Mama was a business school professor at the local university, and sometimes she didn't go to campus until after lunch. So she did the parenting for both her and Baba, which meant she basically yelled for a living, too.

The aroma of green onions and oil made my stomach growl. "Pancakes are ready!" Mama said, setting two plates of pancakes on the table.

Lisa put the cereal back on top of the fridge and sat down at the kitchen table, sulking. I took my seat across from Lisa and inhaled my pancakes in three bites. *Mmmm.* I licked the oil from my lips, wishing I could eat breakfast again.

On the other hand, Lisa took, like, eight hours to eat one baby-sized bite. Then she went right back to taking selfies on her phone.

"Whoa." I noticed the electric-blue eye shadow on Lisa's face. "Where are you going—the first day of clown school?"

Lisa glared at me but then smirked. "Laugh now, while you can, because you won't be laughing for the next three years," my sister said. She jabbed her fork at me, and I dodged the piece of pancake that came flying off it. "Middle school is the armpit of the education system. The good news is, after today, you'll never have another first day of middle school. The bad news is, you'll have to face the misery that is the rest of your life."

Puberty had made Lisa very intense. "Gee, thanks."

"Lisa, stop picking a fight with your sister. Finish your pancake," Mama scolded.

"I'm full," Lisa announced as she pushed back her chair and stood up. "Mama, can you drive me to school?"

"You know I can't," Mama sighed. "Just take the bus."

My sister's face resumed its usual scowl. "Fine. I have to go catch the smelly old bus, or I'll be late."

"Wait—I packed a lunch for you!" Mama grabbed a Tupperware off the counter and shoved it into Lisa's hand.

Scrunching up her nose, Lisa stared at the container like it was a dead rat. "What's this?"

"Mapo tofu and squid. It's good for you."

Lisa set the Tupperware back down on the counter. "I'll just buy something from the cafeteria." She cut a sharp look at me. "And, Winnie, if you know what's good for you, you won't bring this food to school, either."

"I like Mama's cooking," I said, mostly to score brownie points with Mama. But also because it was the truth.

There was nothing in the whole world that tasted better than my mother's home-cooked Chinese food. Mama probably could've been a professional chef if she wanted to.

Culinary talent was something that ran in the family. My grandma on my mother's side had owned a successful restaurant in Shanghai. Even though she passed away before I was born, my parents had told me enough about her that I almost felt like I'd known her in life. A framed grainy black-and-white photo hung over the piano in the living room. It showed my unsmiling grandmother standing in front of her prized restaurant. Whenever I looked up at that photograph, I liked to pretend that she was still watching over our family.

"You're just a brownnoser, Winnie," Lisa muttered, rolling her eyes.

"Am not." I stuck my tongue out at her.

My sister didn't seem to be bothered by my comeback. She probably thought I was childish for sticking my tongue out. "Don't say I didn't warn you about the lunch thing." Shrugging, Lisa swung her new purple backpack over her shoulder and bolted from the kitchen.

"Lisa, get back here!" Mama cried, but the days of her threats working on Lisa had long passed.

The front door slammed. I said a silent prayer for Lisa. I'd heard bad things about middle school, but the things I'd heard about high school were even worse.

"Your sister never wants to eat my cooking anymore," Mama sighed. "When did she become such a picky eater?"

"Probably around the same time she started wearing electric-blue eye shadow." Middle school had changed Lisa a lot, and not for the better.

There was a short silence, and then Mama asked in a sharp voice, "You should get going, too, right? And did you finish all your homework?"

"It's only the first day of school! We didn't get homework," I protested.

"You should have asked for some."

That didn't even make sense. Leave it to Mama to be on my case about work before the school year even officially started.

Whatever. I was determined to have a great first day. And nobody, least of all my crabby older sister or my strict mother, was going to ruin it.

I made it through my first three classes without getting dumped into a trash can or shoved into someone's locker. By middle school standards, I was thriving. No one was doing the first day of school like Winnie Zeng.

Although I recognized a lot of students who'd gone to Groton Elementary School with me, most of my friends had transferred to Stuyvale or some other fancy private school. Making friends all over again was going to be a real grind.

By the time lunch rolled around, I was starving. All I wanted to do was eat the yummy mapo tofu and squid Mama had made last night, which she said had "extra spice to give you extra energy for the first day of school."

As soon as I walked into the cafeteria, I was overwhelmed by the number of people there—mostly new faces. Even the students I recognized from elementary school had evidently decided to remake themselves over the summer. Girls were now wearing lip gloss and eye shadow, and guys had started styling their hair. I was self-conscious of the fact that I was probably the only one who looked the same as their fifth-grade version, except half an inch taller, according to the wardrobe I'd outgrown over the summer.

I stood there for a moment, frozen, unsure of where to go. As I scanned the cafeteria, my gaze landed on a black-haired boy leaning against a pillar near the cafeteria entrance. He wore a white dress shirt paired with a red bow tie and khakis. A pair of circular glasses sat on his nose. He looked like the poster child for uncool.

That wasn't even the worst part. The worst part was that I knew that uncool profile like I knew the periodic table of elements. Like I knew the theme song for *Sailor Moon*.

I almost dropped my lunch box in shock. *"David!"*

This was officially the worst first day of school ever.

CHAPTER TWO

David Zuo turned around, and we locked eyes. A jolt of electricity practically crackled in the air between us.

"Winnie." He didn't exactly look happy to see me, but it wasn't like I was happy to see him, either. In fact, this encounter was sitting at the very top of my Terrible Middle School Memories list, and it was still only the first day. This was going to be a long year.

I marched over to David. "What the heck are you doing in my school?" I couldn't believe this was happening. I was supposed to be the top student of the sixth grade. Having David around was going to make that a lot more difficult.

He made a face. "Since when did this become *your* school?"

"Aren't you supposed to be at Stuyvale?" *Making everyone there miserable?* I added in my head. Stuyvale ran from kindergarten through eighth grade, so if all had gone according to plan, I wouldn't have had to put up with attending the same public school as David until we were both in high school. Trust me, I'd run the calculations many times before.

"Plans changed," David replied evasively. "I had to

transfer to Groton Middle School for . . . um, reasons." His expression twitched, and he cleared his throat, his eyes darting away from mine toward the ceiling.

I followed his gaze upward, but there was nothing there. I stared back at David, who was now looking down at the table as though it were the most fascinating object in the world. Okay, David was acting kind of weird, but I shouldn't have expected anything else from the kid who spent his recesses at Chinese school polishing his abacus.

"What reasons?" I said, eyeing him suspiciously.

David pinned me with a cool stare. "Never you mind. Believe me, I'd much rather be at Stuyvale, too. The school lunches there were exquisite, not to mention all organic." A faraway look entered his eyes, and David pressed his hand to his chest. "My personal favorite was the arugula salad with mixed greens and freshly caught wild Alaskan salmon."

It took me a moment to translate David's words from fancy-pants Stuyvale-speak into plain old English. "Just say 'salad with salmon' like a normal person," I sighed. Private schools were weird. Also, what the heck was an arugula?

"I'm not even sure what *that* is." Nose wrinkling, David pointed down at the soggy, sad-looking slice of cheese pizza on a nearby boy's tray. The boy gave him an offended look and scooted his food away.

"Pizza, David," I explained as though to a much smaller child. "That's pizza. It's what regular eleven-year-olds eat."

"I know. I was being facetious."

Facetious. It was too early in the day to be breaking out the SAT vocab. "Listen, I'm having a good first day, and I don't need anything—or anybody—ruining it. I'm sure you feel the same. So let's just start over with a fresh slate and forget everything that's happened in the past, okay?"

"You mean, like the fact that I beat you by half a point at the piano competition two weeks ago?" David flashed his signature obnoxious smile, as though his superiority were obvious.

"Yes. Stop talking about that, please," I said through gritted teeth.

"Fine. Then should we talk about how last year, I beat you by *two* points at the piano competition?"

"Now you're just bragging!" There it was, that familiar, snooty look on David's face. I slammed a hand down on the nearby cafeteria table, which was a huge mistake. The surface was all sticky and gross, with what smelled like strawberry jam. I closed my eyes and took a deep breath. "I know back at Stuyvale you were the top student or whatever, but around here *I'm* the top student. And I'll be the top student this year, too."

"We'll see about that." David pushed his glasses up on the bridge of his nose. "Also, you have jam on your hand, genius."

My cheeks flamed with embarrassment. This was my cue to make a speedy exit. "A-anyway, I gotta go. Just heard someone calling my name." I hadn't, but maybe someone had actually called my name and David's loud mouth drowned it out. "I'll see you around."

I turned away and headed toward the sanitizer dispenser at the opposite end of the cafeteria. With my hands clean, it was time to push my encounter with David to the back of my mind and turn my attention to the next problem: I had no idea where to sit.

After a quick scan of the cafeteria, I spotted a familiar tall, thin Asian girl wearing her thick black hair in two braids. Relief flooded through me.

It was Allison Tan, a girl from my Chinese school. Allison and I weren't that close, but our moms were friends. There were only a handful of Asian students at Groton Middle School, so I was extra relieved to see a friendly, familiar face. Most important, no one was sitting at the table with Allison, so now I had someone to sit with.

By the way, having a lunch buddy—preferably a whole crew—was really important in middle school. Sitting alone at lunch was a social death sentence, according to Lisa. You might as well shove yourself into your own locker and eat lunch in there.

"Hey, Allison." I sat down at the empty seat to her left and pulled my Tupperware out of my pink *Sailor Moon* lunch box. The smell alone made my stomach growl.

"Winnie," Allison greeted in her soft, timid voice. She smiled, showing off a mouth full of braces. "How was your summer?"

With a piece of squid halfway to my mouth, I froze. This was a pivotal moment. I couldn't mess it up. Whatever I told Allison would get back to her mother, then to their whole circle of Chinese mothers, and eventually everyone else in the world, including the College Board. My whole future was on the line. I had to say something impressive.

I puffed out my chest. "I won the Junior Math Summer Tournament, and I placed second at a piano competition."

"Oh," Allison said, blinking. "Um. Cool. Did you do anything fun, though?"

"Piano and math *are* fun." Even though I didn't actually believe that, I made sure to speak up, just in case Mama or one of her auntie friends happened to be around. Those ladies had eyes and ears *everywhere*. "What did you do?"

"Well, let's see. I went to the pool a lot for swim practice, and the mall—"

"Hey, Allison! You saved us seats?" The next thing I knew, a trio of chattering girls I recognized sat down around us.

Jessamyn, Tracy, and Kim, the popular girls from Groton Elementary School, were clearly not planning to step down from their thrones in middle school. The girls wore matching blue eye shadow and had even painted their nails blue. What was with the color blue this year?

Out of the three, Jessamyn was the most popular. She was the trendsetter, whose long blond hair was always highlighted with a new color every couple of months. Now it had purple highlights. She'd also developed the reputation in the fifth grade of being the meanest in the trio. I'd heard she even made one of the fifth-grade teachers cry. Everyone knew not to mess with Jessamyn.

Tracy had chin-length brown hair and was the quietest. I suspected she was nice, too, and I wasn't sure why she hung around Jessamyn and Kim. One time last year, Tracy helped me pick up some papers when I dropped them in the hall. Then Jessamyn came by and made her drop the papers.

Kim had red hair, and she was like Jessamyn's sidekick, parroting whatever she said. If Jessamyn ever transferred schools, I was pretty sure Kim would be scrambling to grow a personality.

The three girls had bought Caesar salad for lunch, which made me pity them. I could practically hear Mama's voice in my head: *Ten dollars for a handful of lettuce leaves and three croutons? Waste of money!*

"Winnie, these are my friends from the swim team," Allison said. "Girls, this is Winnie. She goes to my Chinese school."

Tracy's eyes flickered toward me, and I thought there might even have been a hint of friendliness in them. "Oh yeah, Winnie. You went to Groton Elementary, right?"

I nodded. I hardly dared to hope, but maybe the girls had changed over the summer. Maybe in the sixth grade, we could be friends—

"Oh my god, what are you *eating*?" Jessamyn asked, covering her mouth with her hand.

"Whatever that is, it smells weird," giggled Kim.

The three girls gawked at my lunch with a mixture of horror and disgust. My cheeks began to burn with embarrassment, and a distant ringing noise entered my ears. If a hole had opened up in the floor and swallowed me right then, I would have been grateful. "Um . . . it's . . . Chinese food."

Jessamyn gagged, and Kim waved her hand in front of her nose like she smelled something putrid. I looked toward Allison for help. Allison had to eat Chinese food all the time, too. She would explain that mapo tofu and squid weren't weird or smelly.

But Allison stayed silent. Her ears were bright red. She stared down at her cafeteria pizza like she wanted nothing more than to melt right along with the cheese on the tray. Allison was embarrassed, I realized. Embarrassed of *me*. Me and my weird lunch.

Suddenly, I understood Lisa's warning from earlier that morning: *And, Winnie, if you know what's good for you, you won't bring this food to school, either.* So that was why she'd stopped eating Mama's home-cooked meals. Chinese food and middle school cafeterias didn't seem to . . . mix.

I put my unfinished meal back into my Tupperware and packed up my belongings. "I'll see you around, Allison," I muttered, barely glancing back at her or the other girls.

My ears burning with shame, I marched out of the cafeteria and past David, who'd sat down next to the kid eating pizza. He stared at me with pity in his expression, which made me feel even worse about my already horrible day. I spent the rest of the lunch hour in the library.

Middle school: 1; Winnie: 0.

"Winnie, is something wrong? You didn't finish your lunch or dinner."

Mama burst into the living room, where I was sitting on the couch, trying to finish my science homework that evening, after the first day had mercifully ended. I didn't look up. From her outraged tone alone, I could picture the annoyed expression on my mother's face.

"I'm not that hungry," I said.

"What? But you're always hungry. Are you sick?" Mama bent down and pressed the back of her hand to my forehead, checking my temperature.

I pulled back. "I'm not sick. I'm just not hungry, okay?"

Ever since lunch, the horrified looks on those girls' faces in the cafeteria had been tattooed on my brain. Now the thought of Mama's home-cooked dinner—wood ear mushrooms and roast duck—wasn't appetizing at all.

"You have to finish your food, Winnie. If you don't, you'll grow up to be short, like your sister."

"Hey, I heard that!" Lisa yelled from the kitchen.

"Yeah, yeah, I got it," I said, just to get Mama to stop nagging me.

"You'd better not let me catch you throwing out food again, or else I'll throw out all your sweets," Mama threatened. "First Lisa, now you. I'm your *mother*. You girls shouldn't think I'm afraid to punish either of you! Nobody takes me seriously in this household."

As if that weren't enough, Baba came home then. Still wearing his suit, he set his briefcase down on the floor with a weary sigh. Mama turned her attention to him, thankfully leaving me alone for a little while.

"Hurry and eat. Dinner's getting cold," she told Baba by way of greeting. She ushered him into the kitchen.

My family didn't really hug and kiss or anything like that. Mama and Baba weren't very emotional or touchy-feely, and neither was Lisa. We weren't like the families I saw on American TV. Sometimes it made me wonder if that meant my family really *was* weird. If we were programmed differently. Sometimes I wondered if we were actually a robot family.

"Winnie, did you practice piano today?" Robot Baba called from the dining table.

"Yeah." Quietly, I groaned. I was never going to get this homework done with my parents nagging me.

"Good. Don't forget your piano recital is coming up."

"That reminds me," Robot Mama interjected. "I ran into Zuo shū shu at the Golden Asia supermarket a few days ago."

Oh brother. Here we go again. Whenever my parents started a sentence with *I ran into such-and-such shū shu* or *ā yí,* it meant a comparison between me and their genius kid was incoming. And 99 percent of the time, said genius kid was David Zuo.

Sure enough: "David Zuo is only one month older than you, and he's already entering level eight for his next piano test," Robot Mama said. "That's a level above you!"

My mood dipped instantly. There had once been a time—we're talking a *really* long time ago, when dinosaurs roamed the earth and it was acceptable to wear Crocs—when I actually *did* enjoy playing the piano. But that was before piano tests. Before David Zuo became my parents' benchmark for child perfection. Before piano became another area where I wasn't good enough.

"You have to work harder," Robot Baba said. "You can't fall behind David."

"You can do better than this, Winnie," added Robot Mama.

"You guys always tell me to work harder, but it's never enough," I muttered under my breath.

"What did you say?"

"Nothing," I called back. If I said my true thoughts aloud, it would just lead to an argument. Lisa was the only one in this house who understood what it was like trying to live up to our parents' ever-growing expectations. Too bad she hardly wanted anything to do with me anymore.

"That means finishing your lunch and dinner, too, Winnie," Robot Mama scolded. "Even Lisa is being good and eating her food." There it was again, the comparison game between my sister and me. "How are you going to get the energy to practice piano if you don't eat your food?"

I grunted in agreement, just to stop all the nagging. It wasn't like I wanted to upset my parents by refusing to take their food to school. In fact, disappointing them was pretty much the last thing I wanted.

But I wanted to fit in at school even more. I had no plans to eat weird lunches there, where the popular kids would make fun of me.

So for the rest of the week, I didn't leave a scrap of food in my lunch box. Instead, I dumped the lunch into the trash and joined Allison and the salad crew in eating bits of lettuce. I was spending my precious allowance and money from New Year's gifts, but I didn't mind. Right now, fitting in was more important than saving money.

Yeah, the school salad was bad. And, yeah, my stomach twisted with guilt whenever I threw out Mama's homemade food. Maybe if I were stronger, braver. Maybe if I were a girl with hidden superpowers, a Sailor Scout, I'd have put those mean girls in their place for saying rude things about Mama's food.

But I was none of those things. Just plain old Winnie Zeng. So I said nothing. At least this way, none of those girls would make fun of me again.

CHAPTER THREE

"All right, class. Settle down," said Mrs. Payton as everyone trickled into homeroom. She held a stack of flyers in her arms. "I have a very exciting announcement today."

"Is the school year ending early?" Parker asked.

"Is the cafeteria finally gonna serve good food?" Jessamyn piped up.

"No and no," said Mrs. Payton. Half the class deflated in disappointment, and I could practically see the shift in the room as students mentally checked out. I felt kinda bad for the teacher. Mrs. Payton pointed at the small boy who sat in front of her desk—Jeremy Miller, the kid who'd impressively already managed to become the teacher's pet. "Jeremy, help me hand out these flyers."

Jeremy practically leapt out of his seat in his eagerness to obey, causing Jessamyn to roll her eyes at Kim, who snickered. Then he went up and down the aisles passing out flyers. I grabbed one from his hand as he walked by my desk.

The flyer read:

GROTON MIDDLE SCHOOL FALL FAIR

SIXTH-GRADE BAKE SALE:
MRS. PAYTON'S CLASS
VS.
MR. BURNSIDE'S CLASS

September 30 from 9 a.m. to 10 a.m.
*All proceeds will be donated to
the World Wildlife Fund.*

Mrs. Payton continued. "The sixth grade will host a bake sale as part of the Fall Fair in two weeks. It's an annual tradition at Groton Middle School. For those of you who need an extra incentive to bake and sell lots of goodies, we'll be in competition with Mr. Burnside's homeroom. The winning class will get a pizza party!" Mrs. Payton threw up some jazz hands, clearly thinking she'd delivered the best news in the world.

Last year, having a pizza party would've been the *coolest*

thing, right behind school getting canceled. But we weren't babies anymore. Now we were middle schoolers, and life was all about being too cool for school.

I looked around at my classmates. Annie Wetz was nodding off. Pranav Jain was throwing spitballs into Melissa Prince's hair.

Mrs. Payton pursed her lips, clearly irritated that my classmates couldn't care less about the bake sale. "Fine. Do you all need another incentive? I'll add an extra incentive," she said. "Mr. Burnside's class has won for the past three years in a row, and he never lets me hear the end of it." She scowled and shook her head. "If you win this competition for me, I'll give everyone *ten* extra-credit points toward your English grade in addition to the pizza party."

I perked up at that, and so did half my classmates. Extra credit? That was something I could get behind. Now I definitely wanted us to win. Because guess who was in Mr. Burnside's class? None other than the devil himself—David Zuo.

If I wanted to be the top student of the sixth grade, I *had* to make sure my class beat David's, that I got the extra credit and a higher grade than his. This was my chance to redeem myself since losing our showdown over the summer. And since he'd finished Chinese school at the top of our class last year, with me behind by just a few points.

"Yes!" I hadn't realized I'd spoken aloud until Jessamyn turned and, snickering, gave me a weird look.

But even her snickers couldn't dampen my mood.

This was my chance. This was my year to finally overtake David—starting with the bake sale.

When I got to the cafeteria for lunch, I made a beeline for David's usual table. He was sitting with Pranav Jain, from my homeroom. Neither of them was speaking, as they were both getting a head start on their homework while eating lunch. Typical.

I ignored Pranav, who ignored me, and waltzed up to David. I waved my flyer under his nose.

"Ow! What's the big idea?" David pulled away from me, rubbing his nose as he glared. "You almost gave me a paper cut."

"Did you hear about the sixth-grade bake sale?"

"Yeah. Complete waste of time, if you ask me. I hope they'll have organic food options for those of us who care about our health as well as our ecosystems." He sniffed.

"Just you, then."

A vein throbbed on David's head. In a frostier voice, he said, "So, what about the bake sale?"

"Your homeroom is competing against mine to sell the most baked goods." I gave him a challenging look.

David's eyes narrowed. "Oh, I see. You want to make a bet on whose class will win." I nodded, and he rolled his eyes. "You're so predictable. When are you going to grow up, Winnie?"

"I *predict* that my homeroom will win," I said, ignoring that slight about growing up.

"Fat chance," David snorted. "When was the last time you won against me in *anything*?"

"Whaddya mean? I beat you all the time, like at . . . um, at . . ." I paused, racking my brain. David had outdone me in the last piano competition. At the end-of-year fifth-grade Chinese school poetry competition, he'd won over me, too. When *was* the last time I'd put David in his place? Oh no. It must've happened so long ago that I couldn't even remember it now. The situation was more dire than I'd realized.

David's grin widened as he watched me struggle to form a retort. "That's what I thought. My class has got this bake sale in the bag, too."

I was going to wipe that smug look off David's face if it was the last thing I ever did. "Ha. I'll make you eat those words *and* our cupcakes." I snapped my fingers. "How about this? If my class wins, you'll do my Chinese school homework for a whole month. If your class wins—even though it won't—I'll do *your* Chinese school homework."

"This is so trivial. What are we, middle schoolers?"

I waited a second for David to realize.

"Oh . . . right." David sighed. With the air of resigning himself to something silly, he stuck out his hand. "Fine. Even though I can think of a million more important things to do, I'll take you up on your ridiculous bet."

"Polishing your abacus doesn't count as important, David."

His cheeks reddened. "I didn't—that—that's only for

special occasions! A-anyway, that's neither here nor there. We have to shake on this bet."

I stared at David square in the eye. Unfortunately for him, Mama had taught me how to shake hands properly when I was in elementary school. That was Business 101, as she called it. A firm handshake was important for establishing dominance.

I grabbed David's hand from above, gripped it tightly, and shook it up and down in a quick, strong motion. Poor boy never stood a chance.

"Ow! What're you trying to do—yank off my arm?" David protested, drawing his arm back and shaking it out.

"That was my Handshake of Doom." The name had come to me on the spot, and I was pretty proud. It was inspired.

"Handshake of—*excuse me?*"

"I look forward to winning the bake sale." And as David was still struggling to devise a comeback, I turned around and walked away quickly, resisting the urge to skip. *Witness my Exit of Victory, David.*

"Dude, she totally got you there," I heard Pranav say to David.

"Oh, shut up," David retorted.

After declaring the bet with David, I got to work as soon as school was over. The house was empty except for Lisa because Mama and Baba were still at work. Lisa might as well not have been home, either. She usually just ignored me and gossiped with her friends on the phone for hours.

It's hard to believe, but once upon a time Lisa and I were super close. That's what happens when you spend your whole childhood trapped in Boredom City, Nowheresville (also known as Groton, Michigan). You're forced to actually talk to your sibling.

There was nothing to do in Groton except mow the lawn, watch paint dry, and complain about how there was nothing to do while mowing the lawn and watching paint dry. On a really ambitious day, I could bike to the local bookstore, the Suntreader, and read comics and manga for hours until one of the managers threatened to kick me out unless I bought something. Lisa and I used to read comics there all the time, everything from Spider-Man to One Piece. We dreamed that one day we'd get to become superheroes, too. We even wrote bad fan fiction together.

That was before Lisa decided comics weren't cool. Now she'd rather play softball, paint her nails while chatting with her friends, or be rude to me. If you ask me, Lisa's more likely to be the super*villain* than the superhero these days. (But don't tell her I said that.)

"Don't forget to practice piano for an hour," Lisa barked from her bedroom, "or else I'll tell on you." Then she slammed the door.

See what I mean? Pure villainy.

"Yes, sister dearest," I muttered. Little did Lisa know that I had absolutely no intention of practicing the piano.

I pulled up a YouTube video of Rachmaninov's Elégie on my phone, cranked the volume up to full blast, and let the music play on loop from the piano. As long as my sister didn't venture downstairs—which she wouldn't, because she persistently avoided breathing the same air as I did—she'd think I was the one playing the piano this whole time. I'd come up with this life hack about two years ago, and my quality of life had improved exponentially since then. At some point I would have to actually practice the piano so I wouldn't totally fail when I had to give a performance, but that could come later. Right now I had something more immediate to focus my attention on—my grade's bake sale.

My gaze traveled upward and landed on the picture of my grandmother. She seemed to be peering right into my soul with that stern look. I couldn't help but feel a tiny twinge of guilt about what I was doing, but I shook it off quickly. It wasn't like the picture of my grandmother could actually *see* that I was slacking on playing piano.

After I was satisfied with my setup, I turned toward the rabbit pen where we kept the family pet, a white rabbit named Jade. Lisa had gotten Jade as a present when she won a piano competition a few years ago, but she'd grown bored with the rabbit after a few weeks. That was fine with me, since she let me have Jade.

I fed Jade a carrot stick from the dish inside her cage. She seemed restless, scurrying from one end of the cage to the other. "You wanna come outta there for a bit?" Even though Jade couldn't understand me, her head bobbed up and down. I scooped Jade's warm body into my arms and headed for the kitchen.

I made myself a quick, nutritious snack by smearing Nutella on a slice of bread. It tasted like chocolate heaven. If I slapped a jar of Nutella on a loaf of bread and sold that at the bake sale, I bet I'd make a *killing*. Mrs. Payton would never allow it, though. Teachers never let us take the easy way out.

I had to practice baking if I wanted to whip up a best-selling concoction on bake sale day. Luckily, cooking and baking with Mama was one of my favorite things to do, so I had some experience already, but I wanted to try something new. I rummaged through our drawer full of recipe books.

The book covers showed a mix of Chinese and American desserts. They were covered with at least an inch of dust. My parents hadn't used the recipes in *ages*. They usually just threw in a pinch of something here and a dash of something there without following any real instructions. Like magic, their dishes always tasted amazing.

I spotted a light at the bottom of the drawer. Strange. After taking out all the other cookbooks, I fished out a very old-looking red book with brown stains on the cover. For a moment, I could've sworn that it *glowed* bright yellow. But when I blinked and stared at it again, it was just a normal old cookbook. I examined it, and nothing seemed out of the ordinary. Must've been a trick of the light.

Running my fingers over the worn cover, I squinted at the gold Chinese characters. With my slightly-worse-than-David's-but-still-decent Chinese, I was able to read what it said: 姥姥的食谱. *Grandmother's cookbook.*

My parents had probably long forgotten about Lao Lao's cookbook. Carefully, I opened it to the first page. There was a picture of a round brown cake with patterns engraved in it, and Chinese characters in the middle. A mooncake. There was even a little paragraph about the story behind the Mid-Autumn Festival, and the significance of mooncakes.

I couldn't read all the characters, but I already knew the gist of the legend of the moon goddess, Chang E, and the heroic archer, Hou Yi. Chang E was a mortal who drank an elixir of immortality meant for her husband, Hou Yi, and she ended up flying all the way to the moon, separating them forever. Mooncakes symbolized family reunion and prosperity and were eaten in admiration of the moon.

I flipped to the next page, and a small red packet fell out of the book. It was labeled ESSENCE OF THE MOON. Curious, I picked up the packet and opened it. Inside was a fine golden substance that smelled like nothing I'd smelled before. The scent was very faint, but it was a little like cinnamon and sugar mixed with something earthy and rainy—something I imagined the stars would smell like.

I tried to turn to the next page of the cookbook, but the remaining pages were stuck together with a sticky brown substance that felt like hardened brown sugar. After giving a few hard tugs, I gave up. There was no way to flip to any of the other recipes in the book.

A bummer, but I'd make do. Learning how to bake mooncakes would be enough fun to last me for a while, anyway.

I read the recipe.

Ingredients:

2 tablespoons vegetable oil

$1/4$ cup golden syrup or honey

$1/2$ teaspoon alkaline water

$1/2$ cup cake flour

$1/2$ cup all-purpose flour

2 cups red bean paste

1 miniature mooncake mold

1 packet essence of the moon

I stared again at the red packet filled with "essence of the moon," whatever *that* meant. No way it referred to essence from the actual moon. How would my grandmother have gotten ahold of the moon itself?

Most likely, *essence of the moon* was code for a special secret family ingredient. Lao Lao had probably labeled it that way to make the whole baking process seem more magical. The thought brought a smile to my face, though the smile faded as I glanced through the recipe again. Dang, just looking at all the steps was enough to exhaust me. Making these mooncakes was going to take me the whole afternoon. No wonder mooncakes were traditionally eaten only once a year.

I gathered all the ingredients, overturning everything in the kitchen in the process. Thankfully, Mama had planned ahead for the Mid-Autumn Festival, so I managed to find everything I needed, including the miniature mooncake mold.

I got to baking as fast as I could. Mama would be home in a couple of hours, and she'd flip out if she saw me using the kitchen, which was supposed to be off-limits when she wasn't around. I whisked together the liquids and then the cake flour and the all-purpose flour and the "essence of the moon." When the dough was formed, I left it in the fridge for twenty minutes. Then I split the dough into twelve pieces, rolled them out, and filled the insides with the red bean paste, my favorite sweet filling. I put the mooncakes into the mooncake mold.

Finally, the cakes were ready to be put into the oven. As I waited for them to bake, I busied myself by cleaning up the mess I'd made, imagining the priceless look on David's face when I won our bet. None of the baked goods would be as sweet as the taste of victory. I was sure of that. I just hoped nobody would think it was weird to bring mooncakes to school. I mean, mooncakes smelled really good, so that wouldn't be a problem. Right?

Something furry and warm rubbed up against my leg. I barely stopped myself from screaming before I looked down and saw it was only Jade.

"Jade! You scared me." Scooping up the rabbit into my arms, I rubbed behind her ears.

The timer dinged. My mooncakes were ready. I set Jade down on the floor and stared at her, hard. She blinked at me. "Stay put. I'm in the middle of something very important, okay?"

I put on the oven mitts and pulled the mooncakes out of the oven. Steam rose from them as I stared. The mooncakes looked kind of . . . well, lumpy and sad. I didn't have time to decorate them with any fancy designs—not if I wanted to finish eating them before Mama got home or Lisa wandered into the kitchen in search of a snack.

According to my grandmother's cookbook, I could store the mooncakes for a couple of days until their surface turned from dry to shiny. Or I could just eat them now, while they were still dry and slightly ugly, since I was hungry. I mean, it's what's on the inside that counts. Right?

I waited for ten minutes to let the cakes cool on the counter. Those ten minutes crawled by, and it was pure agony. I busied myself by refilling Jade's water dish in her rabbit pen.

When the ten minutes were up, I went back to the tray—and gasped. The mooncakes now gleamed, as though they'd already had a day or two to rest. How was this possible?

Maybe the stress of middle school had gotten to me. Maybe I was seeing things. I blinked. Nope. Those mooncakes were still way shinier than they had any business being. Almost as though they carried the real essence of the moon.

Gingerly, I picked one up and bit into it. It was dense, and the red bean paste was super filling. Sweet, but not too sweet. Just like a mooncake should be. Seriously, if this school thing didn't work out, I could be a professional pastry chef, especially since culinary talent ran in the family. Someone get me on *The Great British Baking Show*.

"Hey, that's actually pretty good. . . . No, Jade!"

I watched in horror as I looked back at the mooncakes. The white rabbit had hopped up to the tray and really gone to town on it. Her coat was covered in mooncake crumbles as she nibbled away.

I picked up Jade in a panic, wiping crumbs off her shivering form. As I set her on the floor, a string of questions raced through my mind. What happened when rabbits ate mooncakes? Was red bean paste poison to them, like how chocolate was poison to dogs? Oh no. Was Jade going to *die*? I was about to rush over to my phone and Google *How to give a rabbit CPR*.

But a voice stopped me dead in my tracks. "Winnie. It's me."

I looked up, down, and all around, but there was nobody in sight. Okay. First my rabbit was eating mooncakes, and now disembodied voices were speaking to me. Just a typical day in the life of Winnie Zeng.

Then it hit me. My older sister was pranking me and hoping I'd make a fool out of myself. Well, she'd chosen the wrong day to mess with me. "Lisa, are you playing a joke? Cut it out!"

"It's me, Winnie. It's your grandmother. Lao Lao."

I rushed around the kitchen, trying to find Lisa's hiding spot. Crouching below the kitchen island, I searched the floor. "That's not funny!"

"Look at me. I'm the rabbit!"

"Lisa, *stop*—ow!" I raised my head so quickly that I bumped it into the kitchen island. Pain burst in my head, and stars erupted in front of my eyes.

As I rubbed the top of my head, I heard my sister screeching from all the way upstairs. Too late, I realized my video of Rachmaninov's Elégie had stopped playing.

"Winnie, what the heck are you doing, making all that noise?" Lisa bellowed from the top of the stairs. "I'm trying to have a phone call, and I can't hear anything!"

"Just—um—really excited about piano," I yelled back, crossing my fingers and hoping she'd buy the explanation without coming downstairs. If Lisa came to check up on me now, I was doomed.

"Well, be quieter." A door slammed.

Okay, so Lisa couldn't possibly have been the one speaking to me down here in the kitchen, unless she was the world's best ventriloquist. That left only one possibility.

"Over here, Winnie, you silly girl!"

Slowly, I turned toward the source of the voice, which was coming from the opposite side of the kitchen, near the pantry. Jade was cocking her head at me and tapping her left foot testily. The family rabbit was speaking to me.

CHAPTER FOUR

Middle school life had officially gone from weird to I-must-be-hallucinating. I'd read and watched just about every middle school survival story out there. But none of them had mentioned anything like *this* happening. Had I missed the chapter about pet rabbits suddenly learning how to speak English?

"Okay." I stared at Jade, taking deep breaths to stay calm. There were any number of reasonable explanations for what was happening. Like, I was hallucinating. Or . . . actually, yeah, that was the only one.

"'Okay'? You meet your grandmother for the first time ever, and all you have to say is 'okay'?"

My pet rabbit had referred to herself as my grandmother. I would've found that hilarious if I weren't so thrown off by what was happening. "The rabbit is talking to me. This is fine."

"Excuse me? 'The rabbit'? That's *Lao Lao* to you," snapped Jade irritably, hopping up onto the counter. "You should show more respect for your elders. Haven't my daughter and son-in-law taught you any manners?"

Before I could respond, the rabbit ... changed. Or rather, a silvery, shimmering substance rose out of Jade. It emerged as shapeless smoke at first, but then it took the form of a stern-looking woman. She wore her hair in a bun piled at the top of her head, and a white robe flowed down to her toes. Her eyes were the sharpest part of her. I swear they pierced through me, right into my soul.

Jade went back to rubbing her paws, like nothing had happened. Well, perhaps to her, nothing *had* happened.

Lack of sleep was making me see things. That had to be it. I rubbed my eyes and blinked. The silvery woman was still there. Rubbed them again. Still there. "I'm going to take a nap," I declared to no one in particular.

But before I could leave, the ghostly figure blocked my path. "Don't you recognize me, my granddaughter? It's me—your Lao Lao."

Granddaughter? Lao Lao?

And then realization finally sank in. I'd only seen this ghostly woman in the framed photograph that hung over the piano, and in a few pictures from my parents' very old photo albums. I'd never seen her in real life. But I still recognized her. Of course I recognized her.

"L-Lao Lao?" I whispered, hardly daring to believe my own eyes.

"That's more like it," harrumphed my grandmother.

"Why ... what ... I mean ... Why did you eat my mooncakes?" I blurted out. Of all the questions I could've asked in that moment—*How have you been since, like, death? Are you a ghost? How is this even possible?*—that was the first one that struck me. Not one of my finer moments.

"Well, what else are you supposed to do with mooncakes?" Lao Lao huffed, and then let out a loud burp. "Oops. Excuse me. You could've gone a little easier on the filling, by the way." She pursed her lips and raised her eyebrows at me, her expression suggesting that maybe I wasn't the sharpest crayon in the box. "Don't worry. I left enough mooncakes for you."

That was good to know, but it wasn't the main issue at hand. "H-how are you *here*?" I stammered. My grandmother, who'd passed away. My grandmother, whom I'd only heard about in stories from my mother. She was here now, right in front of the pantry. It shouldn't have been possible. And yet it was happening.

"Why, you summoned me, silly girl. And what a rude summoning it was, I might add," grumbled Lao Lao. "I was in the middle of wrestling a thieving spirit that had stolen the bread I'd baked." She gestured wildly with her hands as though gripping something large in a headlock. "Of course, I was handling the situation marvelously. It was just a lowly class one spirit—"

"A class one spirit?" I interrupted.

"An animal spirit," my grandmother clarified. "Doesn't have much power on its own. And in the spirit realm, class one spirits are often kept as pets by class two and class three spirits."

As though that explanation was supposed to make any sense to me. Lao Lao might as well have been speaking in a foreign language for all I understood.

But before I could ask what *class two* and *class three* meant, Lao Lao plowed on with her story. "Anyway, imagine my surprise when I was yanked out of the spirit realm, *just* as I'd finally gotten the thief in a headlock, and then was transported into the body of a rabbit! It gave me *quite* the shock. But I'm glad you've unlocked your shaman powers. Now I've finally gotten to meet you, my granddaughter." Lao Lao grinned, stepping forward and reaching out a hand as if to stroke my cheek, but then her ghostly hand passed right through me. Her smile faded, turning sad.

I shook my head, still trying to process my grandmother's words. Something about spirits, and different classes, and a spirit realm . . . Yeah, I was very lost. "I . . . I didn't awaken you, Lao Lao. I don't think I unlocked shaman powers, either. I don't even know what that means."

Lao Lao pointed behind me. "You made something from my cookbook, didn't you? And then ate it?"

"Yeah." The sweet aftertaste of the mooncake lingered in my mouth.

"I cast magic on that cookbook before I died and left it with my daughter, knowing that one day the cookbook would fall into your hands. Once you used a recipe from the cookbook and ate the food, it would awaken your dormant sixth sense and unlock your shaman powers. That means also drawing spirits to you—like me." My grandmother flashed a wide smile, as though this were the most natural conversation in the world.

Whoa. I couldn't believe any of this was happening. Me, having a sixth sense? Spirits that were separated into three classes? My dead grandmother coming back to me through my rabbit? This had to be a really weird dream. Maybe it was the fish I'd had for dinner last night, making my mind come up with strange stuff.

I pinched myself, but nothing happened besides the sharp pain shooting up my arm. Okay, so I guess this really *was* happening. Somehow. In the back of my mind, I'd always considered the teeny, tiny possibility of uncovering magical powers, but I didn't really think it would happen. It was just something fun to daydream about during a boring class.

"Why are you pinching yourself, Winnie? You look foolish." Before I could respond to Lao Lao, she continued. "And as much as I want to catch up with you, we don't have much time to waste. There's a lot you need to learn now that you've awakened your powers. As your overspirit, it's my duty to guide you and become your source of power."

I stared at Lao Lao. "Overspirit?"

"Each shaman has one overspirit, usually a spirit who was a shaman in their past life, or a powerful figure from lore. The most powerful shamans are the ones who inherited their abilities through their bloodline—that's you, Winnie. Together, the shaman and overspirit can unlock powers that neither alone could." Lao Lao perked up and sniffed the air, and an expression of alarm crossed her features. "Wait. Do you sense that?"

"Sense what?" Unnerved, I looked around, but the kitchen seemed the same as always. Nothing appeared out of the ordinary.

Then I felt it. A cold, tingling sensation down my spine. Suddenly, the temperature in the house seemed to go down at least ten degrees, as though someone—maybe Lisa—had messed with the thermostat. If she had, she was going to be in for a lecture when our parents got home. Baba was always going on and on about the expense of air-conditioning.

The doorbell rang.

As if my thoughts had conjured her, Lisa came bolting down the steps. If Mama were home, she'd have scolded my sister for rushing around the house like that.

"Coming, Matt!" my sister hollered.

Matt Zingerman, a.k.a. Lisa's secret boyfriend. He was in the grade above her and had no notable talents, unless you count burping loudly as a talent. I didn't know why Lisa was dating him. I mean, my sister wasn't, like, the most perfect teenager ever or anything—not by a long shot—but she could have done a lot better. And he definitely wasn't worth sneaking around behind our parents' backs for.

Matt came by to hang out a few times a week when Mama and Baba weren't home, and I always made sure to avoid him and Lisa whenever that happened. I couldn't explain why, but he just gave me the creeps.

The front door opened. As quietly as I could, I picked up Jade and motioned for Lao Lao to follow me deeper into the kitchen. The entrance filled with the sound of Lisa laughing and greeting her boyfriend.

Once more, that strange cold sensation gripped me. The temperature seemed to lower yet again. Was something wrong with the heating in our house?

"Ugh. I really don't like Matt, and I don't see why Lisa's dating him." I shuddered.

"Evil."

I blinked. "Oh, I mean, his manners need work, but I don't know if I'd call him *evil.* . . ."

My grandmother turned toward me with a stricken expression. "No! I mean, we have to save your sister from the thief."

"I don't think Matt is a th—"

"Not *him.* Remember how I said I was wrestling a class one spirit when you summoned me here?" Without waiting for a reply, Lao Lao continued in a rush, "Well, I suspect the thieving evil spirit came with me from the spirit realm and is now loose in the human world. And that boy with Lisa has just been possessed by the spirit."

As Lao Lao said that, a growl reverberated throughout the house.

CHAPTER FIVE

Either Matt was being even weirder than usual, or Lao Lao was right and we had an evil spirit on our hands. In our very own house.

Mama never let even a speck of dirt cross our front entrance! She was going to be so mad if she ever found out Lisa had let a whole *evil spirit* inside. At the very least, that thing had better not be wearing shoes in this Asian household.

I set Jade down in the corner of the room next to the sink, out of the way of any potential danger.

"Now we've got to come up with a plan, Winnie," Lao Lao said. "Carefully and calmly. We'll have to figure out a clever way to sneak up on this evil spirit. These spirits can be quite tricky to—*Winnie!*"

I'd grabbed the nearest item, a saucepan, and charged out of the kitchen with it. To heck with making a plan. I was going to deal with this evil spirit the way my parents always dealt with unwanted pests, like bugs and door-to-door salespeople—by chasing them out of the house and off the doorstep.

". . . hear that growling just now?" Lisa said in the hallway.

"Oh, that? Um, that was nothing. Just my . . . stomach," came Matt's response.

The sight that greeted me looked like nothing out of the ordinary. Lisa was holding hands with her rugged-looking boyfriend. They both stared at me with reproach, as if wondering where I got the audacity to breathe the same air as they did.

"Oh, you silly, impulsive girl," my grandmother scolded from behind me. "Now we can't sneak up on that foul creature!"

Judging by the fact that Lisa didn't react to Lao Lao's spirit, it seems she couldn't see or hear her. Matt, on the other hand, glowered first at me—and then at my grandmother.

On a normal day, I wouldn't even spare Matt a second glance. But today I looked at him extra carefully. Squinted my eyes like a scientist studying a specimen under a microscope. If Lao Lao was right and I had awakened a sixth sense, then it would come in handy right now.

And then I saw him—or, rather, *it*.

It was like someone had taken the image of a kinda lumpy-looking but average fifteen-year-old boy and overlaid it on top of . . . some beastly thing that had no business being here on planet Earth. A creature with the head of a bear, the fangs of a vampire, and the muscled body of a pro wrestler. The class one spirit's eyes glowed red as it bared its fangs at me.

"L-Lao Lao," I stammered, "I thought y-you said the c-class one spirits weren't p-p-powerful?"

"Compared to the class two and class three spirits, no. But compared to you, an untrained shaman with no skills to speak of yet—yes."

I tried not to be offended by my grandmother's words.

Lao Lao continued, "And *all* spirits become several times more powerful when they combine with humans, like this poor boy here."

Oh, great. Just the news I didn't want to hear. "AHHHHHHH!" I screamed to mask my fright. Then I raised the saucepan, swatting it toward the evil spirit, like I could threaten it away.

"Winnie, what the heck do you think you're doing with that?" Lisa demanded, pointing at the saucepan in my hands. Her eyes were as round as quarters, and she stared at me as though *I* were the threatening presence here. "Stop waving it around. It's dangerous!"

"I'm saving your life!" Lisa could at least be more grateful.

"Saving my *what*?"

"That's not Matt," I said, pointing at the class one spirit, which bared its fangs at me. "He's been possessed by an evil spirit. I know! I have a sixth sense!"

Okay, maybe talking about sixth senses wasn't the best way to get Lisa to listen to me. My sister turned toward the creature, but not before throwing me a disgusted look. She tugged on his arm. "Sorry about Winnie, Matt. She's being even weirder than usual. C'mon. Let's go upstairs."

Matt let out another long, low growl. This time even Lisa couldn't explain away his odd behavior.

"Um . . . Matt?" She peered at him in concern.

"I haven't stepped foot on Earth in over fifty years," said the class one spirit. Its voice turned distorted and evil-sounding. "Fifty years without being able to eat a single human, before the doors to the human realm were open to me once more."

Oops. Was that my fault?

"I'm starving. And you lucky humans get to be the first ones I feast on. Consider it an honor!" The class one spirit swelled in size, growing until it nearly hit the ceiling. It no longer resembled Matt. The spirit took on the frightening appearance of a cross between a bear and a pig. Its body was covered in brown fur. It had sharp claws and teeth, paired with large, flat ears and the squashed nose of a pig.

I froze. Suddenly, it occurred to me that maybe the saucepan wasn't the best weapon of choice against a beast of this size. I needed a bigger, more threatening weapon, something like a—

"Get the mooncakes, Winnie!" Lao Lao yelled at me.

"Wh-what?" I spluttered. "Mooncakes? I was thinking more like a bazooka, or maybe—"

"STOP BEING A DOLT AND DO AS I SAY. NOW!"

I was too terrified to do anything but obey. First I grabbed my sister by the arm and dragged her toward the kitchen.

Lisa was gazing at her boyfriend in utter shock, like he'd

just transformed into . . . well, a giant evil spirit. "B-but . . . but . . . ," she kept stammering.

"The mooncakes—quickly!" my grandmother hollered. She was zooming ahead of me into the kitchen, following Jade, who'd streaked away from the sink. "And get a jar or some other container that you can use to capture the spirit!"

I didn't see how a spirit that huge could fit in any jar, but there wasn't any time to ask questions. "Here, take these, Lisa!" I swiped a handful of now-cool mooncakes from the baking sheet and stuffed them into my sister's hands. Then I grabbed a mason jar from the drying rack next to the sink and sprinted back into the chaos.

A roar, followed by the sound of glass smashing in the hall. There went Mama's precious vases. Oh, we were so dead. We were going to die twice. Once at the hands of the evil spirit, and the second time at the hands of an angry mother.

With my free hand, I grabbed a couple of the mooncakes. Even at this moment, knowing what we were about to do, I couldn't help but think, *What a waste of food.*

"Wh-what are we supposed to do with these cakes?" Lisa squeaked.

"Good question." I turned toward Lao Lao for help.

"Feed them to the spirit," my grandmother said.

"We feed them to the spirit," I relayed to Lisa.

Confusion was written all over my sister's face, but there

was no time for either of us to question my grandmother's orders. The spirit lumbered into the kitchen. It swiped sharp claws across the kitchen island, breaking open a bag of flour and spilling it all over the floor.

"Eat this!" I pelted a mooncake at the evil spirit's open mouth. Luckily, the many snowy Chinese school recesses I'd spent chucking snowballs at David had sharpened my aim. The mooncake soared through the air and landed right on the spirit's huge purple tongue. The creature swallowed the cake.

We all watched, transfixed with horror, as the class one spirit shuddered. Its skin began turning red, as though it had been burned. The spirit let out another roar, but this one wasn't quite as loud. It sounded more like a roar of pain, like the creature was having a massive bellyache after ingesting the mooncake.

"Dang. Are my mooncakes really that bad?" I said.

"That's a good sign, Winnie," Lao Lao hissed. "It means the enchanted mooncakes are doing their job. Give it another one. This spirit isn't very powerful. One or two more mooncakes should force it to leave that poor boy's body, and the spirit will be weakened enough that you can capture it in the jar."

I obeyed, tossing another mooncake at the spirit. Unfortunately, the creature had learned its lesson, and batted the mooncake away. The dessert sailed out of the kitchen and out of sight.

An idea struck me. "Lisa! Throw your mooncakes, too. It can't bat them all away at once."

Lisa nodded, looking terrified. But my sister wound up her arm and let a mooncake fly. Dang, could my sister throw like a champ. I guess she hadn't been captain of the girls' softball team in middle school for nothing.

The class one spirit slapped away the mooncake and swiped its claws through the air. I dodged them, but just barely. The sharp claws raked the spot where I'd just been standing, catching the end of my shirt. Before the class one spirit could attack again, I chucked another mooncake. This time, the cake flew right into the spirit's open mouth.

You'd think this creature would learn to keep its mouth shut, but I guess all the growling and roaring and making evil noises was more important to it than, oh, not being destroyed.

The spirit hissed and shrank right before our eyes. But it wasn't finished. It snapped its head toward us, and I shuddered when I saw its red eyes glowing with fury.

And I was out of mooncakes. But my sister was still clutching one more.

"Lisa! Finish it off!"

She obeyed, winding up and then throwing with all her might. The motion of an all-star softball pitcher.

The spirit didn't have a chance against her deadly aim. The mooncake shot into its mouth. One more shudder, then a horrible hissing noise, and the spirit exploded in a cloud of dust and smoke. As the smoke dissipated, I could see that a small greenish wisp remained behind, hanging in the air.

"Get it, Winnie!"

I was way ahead of Lao Lao. I swooped in with my jar and caught the wisp inside it, then sealed the lid shut.

CHAPTER SIX

When I'd woken up this morning, I definitely didn't have *battling an evil spirit* on my middle school to-do list. It was just like all my favorite anime shows had predicted: life as an official middle schooler was getting really weird really fast.

Even though the class one spirit had been captured in the mason jar, the creature had left debris in its wake. I tried not to breathe in the dust that lingered in the air. *Great.* Another mess to clean up before Mama got back.

There was a more pressing matter at the moment, though. Collapsed on the floor where the spirit had stood just moments earlier was none other than Matt Zingerman. He appeared unharmed, as well as unconscious. Hopefully, when he woke up, he'd have no idea what had happened.

I looked down at my jar and gasped. "The spirit—it's disappeared." The mason jar was empty.

"Ah, yes, as I said before, that was just a lowly class one spirit," my grandmother explained. "If it hadn't latched on to that boy, it would've been quite easy to get rid of it. If class one spirits don't attach themselves to a strong human host, they'll end up eventually disappearing and regenerating in the spirit realm. It's when the spirits *do* successfully combine with humans that we have problems—which is why your role as a shaman is to capture them at all costs."

Oh boy. This shaman business was starting to sound like a lot of work. Dangerous work. Now I was really regretting that Mama and Baba hadn't let me buy that sword on eBay.

My grandmother's face scrunched up in concentration, as though she was puzzling out something. "Normally, class one spirits wouldn't go after a shaman of their own accord like this," she murmured. "They're typically harmless unless provoked, and not smart enough to even cross over to the human world on their own—not without a class three spirit commanding them. I suppose this one could be an outlier, but . . ." She continued to mutter to herself.

"Lao Lao? What's the matter?"

My grandmother blinked at me and then shook her head, giving me a tight-lipped smile. I recognized that smile. It was the one grown-ups liked to use when they didn't want kids to worry about something that we should *definitely* worry about.

"Never mind. Just thinking aloud."

"Why did that class one spirit attack us?" I asked.

"Well, in general, there's been a lot more spirit activity lately due to the Mid-Autumn Festival," my grandmother explained, lips pursed. "During special times like holidays or other events, people tend to gather and tell stories to one another. Storytelling is the source of power for spirits of all kinds, both the bad and good. We're able to exist in some form as long as the living keep our memory alive. As the Mid-Autumn Festival approaches, the spirits associated more closely with the legends of this holiday will grow in power. That's one of the main reasons why the Spirit Council wants to strengthen shaman protection right now."

That was a lot of new information to digest, but it made sense to me. Lao Lao's memory had been preserved well in my family, and even her cookbooks had been passed down. No wonder she was still thriving in the spirit realm. There had to be spirits even more famous than my grandmother who were a heck of a lot more powerful, too. I just hoped none of those spirits were evil.

"Anyway, we'll have to be on guard for more spirit attacks, as this will most certainly not be the last," my grandmother warned. "My guess is that a far more capable spirit—likely a class three—sent that class one spirit after us."

That definitely sounded like something to worry about. "You think there's a class three spirit on the loose in Groton?"

"It's likely, yes. That's why we need to get you caught up to speed with training. But the class one spirit is gone now, at least."

I gulped and nodded, trying my best not to reveal how nervous I was on the inside. If that had been a class one spirit, then I really didn't want to have to face down class two and class three spirits.

Lao Lao sighed in relief, wiping some nonexistent sweat off her forehead. Then she scowled. "Well, that was certainly not good for my heart. If I weren't dead already, I might have died just now from all the suspense of the moment!"

"Tell me about it," I mumbled, plopping down on the nearest chair and catching my breath. That had been enough excitement to last me for the next decade. "You good, Lisa?" When my sister didn't respond, I raised my head to look at her.

Lisa stood there with a blank expression on her face. She was totally zoned out.

I jumped from my seat and waved my arm in front of her. "Helloooooo? Is anyone home?"

Shaking her head, Lisa blinked and then stared at me with surprise on her face. "Winnie. When did you get here?"

I stared in confusion. Lisa stared right back. "Um, I've been here this whole time?"

"Huh? What are you talking about?"

Lisa was acting even stranger than normal. Maybe the fumes from her nail polish had finally gotten to her head.

"What are *you* talking about? We just took down an evil spirit together, remember?" I pointed down at Matt, who was still out cold on the floor. "A spirit that possessed Matt?"

Lisa's expression turned to shock, as though she was noticing her secret boyfriend's presence for the first time. Her face drained of color. She flung herself to the floor beside him and began shaking his shoulders. "Omigosh. Matt! Mattikins! Why are you on the floor? Are you okay?"

Mattikins. I was going to vomit.

More important, I got a sinking feeling that Lisa's

memories of the event had somehow been wiped. That I was the only one who remembered her boyfriend had been possessed by a class one spirit. That I was the only one who remembered the awesome sister-team moment we'd shared as we took down the bad guy.

That was more sibling bonding than my sister and I had had in . . . I didn't even know how long. For a moment, I think I even *liked* her.

"Unfortunately, Lisa won't remember the events that just transpired. Shamans are the only humans who are able to retain memories of spirits and their magic," Lao Lao explained, as though she'd read my mind. Maybe she had. "Her memories disappeared as soon as the spirit fled."

Lisa was probably going to blame me for the broken vases in the hallway. Great.

Lisa bent down and shook Matt's shoulders. He stirred feebly and then sat up after a moment, rubbing his eyes.

"What happened?" Matt mumbled. "Why am I on the floor?"

"I have no idea. Did you fall asleep?" Lisa asked. "You've been pushing yourself way too hard these days."

Feeling awkward, I tried to join the conversation. "Working hard? Do you work part-time somewhere?" I asked Matt politely.

Lisa threw me a snide "Are you really talking to us" look, which made me shrink back. "No, Matt's just having difficulty with math class."

"Darn . . . equations . . . ," Matt moaned, rubbing his head.

Lisa clearly didn't want me talking to her and her boyfriend. She put her hands on her hips and gave me a scrutinizing look, which I recognized all too well. That was Lisa's "I'm telling Mama" face.

"Also, you should be practicing the piano," she said, her face all pinched up, making her look ten years older. "And were you baking something in here? You know you're not allowed to do that."

"I won't tell if you don't tell," I said, which was basically my standard comeback whenever Lisa threatened to tattle on me (something that occurred at least once a day). After all, pretty much nothing I could do—short of, like, burning the house down—would be worse to our mother than Lisa sneaking around with a secret boyfriend, especially a secret boyfriend who wasn't Chinese. Mama had very strict rules about who we were allowed to eventually date.

"Ugh. Fine." Rolling her eyes, my sister turned her attention away from me and back to Matt. Cooing at him, she helped him out of the kitchen. He was blubbering something about polynomials now.

"Oh dear," said Lao Lao as Lisa left.

"Yeah, Matt's kind of a lost cause—"

"Not the boy," my grandmother interrupted. "I meant, you and your sister don't get along very well, do you? That's quite sad."

I shrugged, looking down at my feet. For some reason, it was hard to meet Lao Lao's gaze now. "I'm used to it." I'd be lying if I said that the fighting between Lisa and me had never upset me, but it was just one of those things that I'd learned to live with.

"Sisters shouldn't fight," my grandmother said.

"Well, spirits shouldn't mess up the house and eat all my mooncakes, and yet here we are," I retorted.

Lao Lao's words had hit home, though. Sisters shouldn't fight as often as Lisa and I did. And we'd once been the kind of tight-knit pair who almost never fought. Lisa was the trendsetter, and I'd follow her around. We did everything together—piano lessons, long family road trips, even figure-skating lessons. (The lessons didn't last long, since we proved quickly that we had no aptitude for the sport.) We watched movies and read books together and could finish each other's sentences. We were practically the same person.

Then Lisa went to middle school and . . . changed. Now we hardly did anything together. We didn't even talk much anymore.

Blinking back tears, I shook my head. Now wasn't the time to think about my sister. Now was the time to do some major cleaning.

I stared around at the mess in the kitchen. There was flour everywhere. But there was an important matter to discuss first, before cleaning. "Earlier you said that my shaman abilities come from my bloodline," I said, turning to Lao Lao. "What exactly does that mean?"

"I was a shaman, too, when I was alive. You hail from a long line of shamans. The power skips every other generation and is passed down to the youngest child in the family. That means that after me comes you."

I didn't know anything about shamanism except from that one time last year when Mark Zhu from my Chinese school tried to convince the teacher that he couldn't finish his homework 'cause he'd been too preoccupied with his "shaman duties." (Those "shaman duties" turned out to be attending a Smash tournament all weekend.)

"Being a shaman means that you serve as a medium between the spirit world and the human world," Lao Lao explained, correctly interpreting the blank look on my face.

That actually sounded . . . neat. Not to mention, it would be a cool activity to put on my college applications. Except nobody would believe me. I mean, *I* barely believed me, and this was all happening *to* me.

A wave of dizziness rushed to my head as I struggled to process the facts before my eyes, and I forced myself to sit down on the floor. "Cool. Cool cool cool cool."

"Winnie? It's okay if you need a moment. I know this is a lot of new and, um, *surprising* information to handle. When my grandmother told me, I fainted and didn't wake up for a full day. . . ."

I took a few deep breaths, willing myself not to faint. *One Mississippi, two Mississippi, three Mississippi . . .*

Then, right before *four Mississippi,* an exciting idea hit

me. I shot to my feet so fast that my head spun. Lao Lao gave me a look full of concern. "Does that mean I basically have superpowers?"

"Superpowers?" Lao Lao repeated blankly.

"Yeah, superpowers. Like how Spider-Man can climb walls and swing from building to building! Or how Supergirl can fly through the air—"

"This isn't a silly comic book, Winnie," my grandmother scolded. "Now that you've awakened your own powers, as well as the spirit realm, you have to take your shaman responsibilities seriously."

"Yeah, yeah, I know," I mumbled. I wondered if shamans were magical enough to be part of the Sailor Scouts in *Sailor Moon*. I wondered if Marvel was hiring shamans. "What exactly are my responsibilities?"

Lao Lao fixed me with a stern look, pursing her lips. "There are three main responsibilities of being a shaman, which you'll need to memorize. One: never unleash any spirits, good or evil, on purpose. Two: in case you accidentally unleash or encounter an evil spirit—which should never happen if you follow the first rule, but just in case—it is your duty to defeat the spirit and therefore return it to the spirit world. And three: you must never let any human discover that you are a shaman." My grandmother crossed her arms over her chest. "If you do your job well, nobody will discover the existence of the spirit realm or the fact that you're a shaman. Otherwise"—a dark shadow loomed over Lao Lao's face—"with humans aware of the existence of this other realm, they'll grow fearful. The spirits in turn will be drawn in by that fear and become more likely to cross into the human world. That will lead to chaos."

So, basically, I was like Wonder Woman . . . if no one knew about Wonder Woman's existence. The superhero the world needed . . . but didn't even know it needed.

No offense to my grandmother, but this gig sounded terrible.

"Sounds like a lot of thankless work," I grumbled. I knew all about thankless work. For every group project last year, I'd been the group leader, doing pretty much everything on my own. Then, at the end, the whole group had shared the credit for *my* work.

"The thanks you receive is that evil spirits don't destroy the world and that everyone gets to continue living under the delusion that they're at peace," said my grandmother.

Well, if I couldn't have my own comic-book series, I guess world peace was the next best thing.

"So how are we going to track down spirits? How do I control my powers? Are you going to teach me?" I asked eagerly, bouncing up on my toes.

"Whoa, slow down, Winnie." Lao Lao held up her hands. "We'll take things one at a time. You won't really have to track spirits—they'll likely come to you, since your powers have awakened, and your magic stems from the combination of stories and food. It's a powerful combination, you know. Many spirits will try to take your cookbook—or, heaven forbid, even possess you—to steal some of that magic for themselves."

Great. Just what I wanted to hear, that I was a walking magnet for chaotic spirits.

Lao Lao continued without noticing my discomfort. "These spirits will grow in power as we approach the Mid-Autumn Festival, and they are more likely to escape from the spirit realm and cross over to the human world during the holidays."

"Why is that?"

"The evil spirits' goal is to cause as much destruction as possible, and there's no better time than when human emotions are running high," said Lao Lao. "These spirits feed off chaos. The more chaos they absorb, the more powerful they become. Once they're powerful enough, they'll cross over to the human world and seek out human hosts to possess—and that's the worst-case scenario. Our job is to make sure that doesn't happen. Now that I'm here, I won't leave unless you want me to. And I don't plan on leaving until I've trained you to be a competent shaman. It's part of my job description."

"Your job description as my grandmother?" I asked. I was pretty sure shaman training wasn't part of the normal grandparent manual, but I could have been mistaken. I hadn't really grown up with grandparents around.

"No, as a shaman recruiter."

"A . . . a *what*?"

"Besides my new task to serve as your overspirit, I work

as a shaman recruiter. That reminds me—take a pamphlet."
Lao Lao fished a packet out of her sleeve and handed it to
me. It looked like one of those brochures Mama and Baba
sometimes got in the mail. There were pictures of people
who appeared to be slightly older than me with their arms
crossed over their chests, flashing black badges on their
chests that read SHAMAN TASK FORCE.

The pamphlet read:

Are YOU a new shaman-in-training?
Just discovered your magnificent new powers?
Hoping to make a positive impact on the world?

The Shaman Task Force wants YOU . . . to protect the
human and spirit worlds!

Made up of the most elite and highly trained shamans
around the world, the fifty members of the Shaman
Task Force are hand-selected by the Department of
Supernatural Record-Keeping, overseen by the Spirit
Council. As a member, you would keep the peace
between worlds, sending escaped spirits back to their
stories in the spirit realm.

To learn more, contact the
Department of Supernatural Record-Keeping at
mmm.supernaturalrecordkeeping.com.

Phone: S-888-888-T-
8888888888888888888881-F

"M-M-M?" I said, staring at the website address. "Not W-W-W, as in 'World Wide Web'?"

"It's the Morld Mide Meb in the spirit realm," explained Lao Lao.

"But those aren't real words," I protested. "At least, not in English. And there's no way this is a real website."

My grandmother ignored me and simply said, "Any other questions?"

I also was confused by the unnecessarily long phone number, but maybe I'd ask about that another time.

Even though the idea of training to be part of something called the Shaman Task Force was intimidating, the thought of my grandmother's presence filled me with happiness. Having Lao Lao by my side, when I'd spent all my life believing she was gone forever? This was the best news. I'd finally get to ask her all the questions I had about cooking, about running her own restaurant in Shanghai. This was my chance to have my grandmother in my life.

"You can take some time to think this over," said Lao Lao, as though she'd noticed the mixture of confusion and concern on my face. "I know it's a big decision to train toward joining the Shaman Task Force, and there are no guarantees that you'll make the cut—but I believe in you. You are my granddaughter, after all." My grandmother's stern expression made it clear that she was expecting me to agree, no matter what she might say. I recognized that familiar look, because it was the same one Mama had every time she gave me the "option" of saying yes or no to cleaning the dishes. (I'd never replied no; I was too scared to find out what might happen to me if I did.) "Joining the Shaman Task Force is an honor of a lifetime, though—one that I took up and that I hope to pass on to you."

Yup. That was definitely expectation in Lao Lao's expression. Now I knew for sure where Mama got her strictness and high expectations from.

"Agh," I managed to say, which caused my grandmother's eyebrows to raise. Oops. Not exactly the most eloquent reply.

"We can discuss more later. Your very first task is to clean up this kitchen," Lao Lao said, throwing me an admonishing look, as though *I* were the evil spirit who'd made a mess here. "We can't possibly train in a messy kitchen."

I sighed. "Yes, Lao Lao."

Lao Lao helped me clean, even using some magic to help repair the vases. My jaw dropped when she waved her hand over the smashed glass and it formed into two perfectly shiny vases once more. "Whoa! Can you teach me how to do that?"

"Unfortunately, no. Your powers as a shaman are limited to being able to call upon spirits. You're still bound by your human shortcomings," my grandmother said patiently.

My shoulders sagged. Imagine all the fun I could've had if I could do magic. Imagine all the pranks I could pull on David.

A sudden thought struck me as I remembered the earlier

fight in the kitchen. "Wait. How come Lisa was able to see the evil spirit but she can't see you, Lao Lao?"

"Evil spirits are made out of chaos, and chaos is much easier for the naked human eye to detect," my grandmother explained. "On the other hand, humans tend to overlook the good spirits, which contain very little chaos. Human beings always latch on to the bad rather than the good. That's just human nature, after all."

I thought about the awful stuff I saw on the news all the time, and on Twitter and YouTube. Yeah, Lao Lao's words made sense. News stories about people behaving badly *always* went viral.

The house was spotless by the time Mama's car pulled into the garage. As usual, Matt left by climbing out Lisa's window and down the drainpipe. Lisa, carrying her textbooks and acting like she'd been studying them all afternoon, came downstairs.

When Mama entered the living room, she gave Lisa and me an exhausted smile. Jade was curled up in my lap. Lao Lao floated above, unseen by her daughter and elder granddaughter.

To my mother, we were the perfect picture of a serene, average suburban family.

"Had an eventful afternoon?" Mama asked absently as she hung her coat on the coatrack.

"Not at all," Lisa and I chorused.

CHAPTER SEVEN

As a precaution moving forward, I decided I was going to avoid kitchens, a.k.a. danger zones where spirits could attack, forever. Okay, maybe not *forever*. Maybe till I was fifty. I was at least going to avoid them until I graduated from high school and left this town, which was as good as forever anyway.

But that's so drastic, Winnie, you might say.

You know what *I* think is drastic? The spirit of my grandmother leaping out of my pet rabbit, an evil spirit nearly rampaging through my home, the existence of a spirit realm—and the fact that I was somehow a *shaman*. These were drastic times in the life of Winnie Zeng, and drastic times called for drastic measures.

The next morning, I spent a solid five minutes lying in bed and staring at the ceiling. I still wasn't sure my epic battle with an escaped spirit hadn't been a product of my overactive imagination in my sleep. My grandmother's spirit, floating above Jade, stirred awake. Since Jade and Lao Lao were linked, I was going to have them both sleep in my room from now on.

"Good morning, Winnie," said my grandmother sleepily.

"Good morning." As I rubbed my eyes and yawned, my gaze fell on Lao Lao's pamphlet on my bedside table. Further proof that yesterday hadn't been a very strange dream.

Last night I'd gone to the web address listed on the pamphlet, and found the Shaman Task Force website. There wasn't a whole lot of information available, nor could I find a straightforward application process for becoming a member. I tried searching *Shaman Task Force* on Google, but didn't find anything there, either. Not that I'd really expected to.

All the pamphlet and website told me was that a shaman-in-training would have to successfully capture a class one, two, *and* three spirit before even being *considered* by the mysterious Spirit Council. That was all I needed to know to realize that this shaman-training business was going to be a whole lot of work.

"What's wrong?" my grandmother asked.

I guess all my heavy thoughts must've shown on my face. "I'm still confused about this Shaman Task Force stuff."

"You don't need to concern yourself with the specifics of the Shaman Task Force just yet," my grandmother sniffed. "The Spirit Council will be in contact with further details if you pass the initial screening by catching a spirit from each class. And so far you've only managed to catch one, and very narrowly, I might add. Focus on your training first. Right now, you would be laughed right out of the organization if you tried to join."

The worst part was, I couldn't even argue with Lao Lao,

because she was right. I had no idea what I was doing. If I wanted to capture a class two and eventually a class three spirit, I needed to level up a lot. And I was determined to get there. I didn't want to let my grandmother down.

Plus, there was no denying that a big part of me—the part that was Lao Lao's granddaughter—was intrigued by the idea of joining a Shaman Task Force. I'd just discovered that I had powers and that there was a whole world of spirits that existed beyond the human world. This was some real-life Marvel-like stuff. Peter Parker had nothing on me.

"Are there also different classes of overspirits, like how there are three classes of other spirits?" I asked my grandmother.

Lao Lao shook her head. "No. Overspirits are the spirits of those who were once human, and unless it's to partner with a shaman, we see no reason to cross over into the human world. We overspirits don't feed off chaos, so there's no point. But the class one, class two, and class three spirits *do* feed off human destruction. They aren't necessarily evil in the spirit world, but by taking in the chaos of the human world, they grow more evil here. If left unchecked, they could cause disturbances in the spirit and human worlds that would ultimately lead to the collision and destruction of both. That's why it's so important to keep these worlds and their inhabitants apart."

I'd learned so much already, and it wasn't even eight a.m. yet. Still, I had so many more questions to ask my grandmother.

"You should get going, shouldn't you?" Lao Lao raised an eyebrow. "You'll be late for school."

"Oh—right!" I'd gotten so wrapped up in thoughts of shaman training that I'd almost forgotten.

After leaping out of bed in a frenzy, I washed my face and brushed my teeth in record time. Then I ran down the stairs fast enough to put the Flash to shame.

"WINNIE! BREAKFAST TIME," Mama yelled right on schedule.

Since I'd decided I would never set foot in the kitchen again, I ignored her shouts and made a beeline for the front door instead. No way was I risking anything supernatural happening today. "Sorry, I'm running late!"

"What? Did you at least remember to bring your homework?"

"Of course!" As if I could forget, with Mama and Baba nagging me about my work all the time.

My gray Pusheen backpack had an emergency snack stash—hey, you never know when you'll get hungry—so my plan was to eat a granola bar on the bus. Hopefully, my Nature Valley crunchy peanut butter bar wouldn't summon any demons or spirits of my ancestors.

Speaking of spirits of my ancestors, I cast a look at Jade's rabbit pen in the living room as I ran out the door. Yep, there was Lao Lao's spirit, still hovering above my pet rabbit, now fast asleep. She was snoring with her mouth open while hovering sideways in midair.

With that, my hopes that yesterday's events had been a strange dream were officially dashed. Oh well. But since Lao Lao was here to ward off any bad spirits (at least when she was awake), I didn't have to worry about them causing a ruckus while I was away at school. I ran to catch the bus, and instantly rain began to pour from the gray clouds overhead.

Great. Off to a good start so far.

At school, I had to deal with a double whammy of evil that had nothing to do with the supernatural: David and PE class.

By the way, PE is the worst idea for a middle school class ever. You've got the bigger kids who've gone through puberty dunking on the smaller kids who haven't even hit their growth spurt yet. And then, after the torture of PE ends, you get to go to the rest of your classes all sweaty and beat up.

Today in gym class we were playing dodgeball. David went out of his way to chuck as many dodgeballs at me as he could, and I returned the favor. Eventually, one of David's dodgeballs smacked me right on my thigh.

"Ow! You threw that hard on purpose!" I yelled, raising my voice to make sure the teacher, Mr. Nichols, heard me.

"You're out, Zeng," Mr. Nichols said without even looking up from his clipboard.

I scowled. Some shaman I was—I couldn't even defeat David in a dodgeball game. David stuck out his tongue at me as I stomped off to sit on the sidelines with the other kids who'd gotten themselves eliminated. I spent the rest of the class period dreaming up ways to get back at David. Why was Lao Lao so concerned about evil spirits when there were goobers like David on the loose?

During homeroom, Mrs. Payton had reminded us that the whole school was getting ready for the Fall Fair and told us to start thinking about what we'd like to bring in for the bake sale. I'd been so preoccupied with homework and trying not to freak out over the fact that *I was a shaman* that the bake sale had slipped my mind. I mean, could you blame me?

To top it all off, we started our first unit in Mrs. Lee's English class—mythologies. And with a new unit came a boatload of new work.

"For the next two months, we'll be learning about all different kinds of mythologies throughout the world," she said, her eyes growing huge with excitement behind her round red glasses. "Greek, Egyptian, Japanese, Chinese . . ." As Mrs. Lee spoke, she wrote each word on the whiteboard. Her short brown curls bounced with each movement. "And—oh yes, Winnie, do you have a question?"

Winnie. That was me. I jolted out of my sleepy, almost-napping state. "I—I wasn't sleeping!" I blurted out in panic. Then I clapped my hand over my mouth. The class giggled, and my cheeks burned. *Good one. You totally fooled them all.*

But Mrs. Lee wasn't even paying attention to me. Her

73

gaze was on Megan Kim, who had her hand raised on the other side of the room and now was frowning in confusion. "Um . . . I'm not Winnie. I'm Megan."

Mrs. Lee's mouth parted in surprise, and then she let out a short, embarrassed laugh. "Oh, my mistake! So sorry. What did you want to ask, Megan?"

As Megan rattled off her question, my annoyance grew. It was only the beginning of the year, so I guess it was understandable that Mrs. Lee would still be mixing up students' names. But I didn't see her messing up with any *other* kids' names.

Megan was the tallest girl in class and had long, dark brown hair, which she always wore up in a high, sleek ponytail. I was one of the shortest girls in class, and I usually wore my long black hair in two braided pigtails. In other words, Megan and I looked *nothing* alike. Maybe Mrs. Lee was overdue for her next eye exam.

"For your first big project in this unit, each of you will prepare a report about a specific legend from one of the world's mythologies, which you'll present to the class. If you'd like, you may partner up for the presentation," Mrs. Lee said, to a collective groan. "It'll be fun!"

Our teacher probably needed to update her definition of *fun*. I hated presentations, and I could tell from the groans in the classroom that I wasn't the only one who felt that way. The idea of getting up in front of my classmates, feeling their stares on me, made me want to crawl under my desk and never come back out. Given the choice between doing a presentation and fighting off an evil spirit, I'd take the evil spirit.

Something told me Mrs. Lee wouldn't find that an acceptable substitute for her assignment, though. Teachers like to take all the fun out of education.

When I returned home from a very long day at school, my plan was to act like everything was as normal as before, and power through my mountain of homework. As Mama and Baba always said, getting good grades in school was extremely important. And I didn't want to let them down.

Unfortunately, Lao Lao had other ideas.

My grandmother's spirit swarmed me almost the moment I stepped through the front entrance. "Where were you all day, Winnie?" Lao Lao demanded, crossing her arms over her ghostly chest.

"There's this thing called school," I grumped, dropping my heavy backpack with a *thud* that shook the wood-paneled floor. "Maybe you've heard of it. I have to be there for eight hours every day."

"Don't sass me, young lady! Even when you're at school, you have to be vigilant with your shaman training. In fact, I insist that you take me with you to school from now on, so I can guide you there as well. You never know when evil will strike—especially if there really is a class three spirit roaming in Groton, as I suspect."

"What? I can't bring you to class," I spluttered. Bringing Lao Lao to school would mean bringing Jade to school, too, since they were linked. Maybe there wasn't anything specific against bringing the spirits of grandmothers to class in my middle school handbook, but there were *definitely* rules against bringing animals into the classroom. "Pets aren't allowed in school."

"I'm not a pet—I'm your grandmother!"

"Well, spirits of grandmothers aren't allowed, either, probably. I'd get kicked out!"

Lao Lao pursed her lips. "Use your clever brain and figure out a way to sneak us in. This is more important than school rules."

"I thought there was nothing more important than school." Mama and Baba and all the Asian aunties and uncles in the whole universe certainly thought that way.

"We still have to train you. Evil won't rest simply because you're in math class."

"Evil *is* math class," I muttered.

"You have to be vigilant, Winnie," said my grandmother stubbornly.

"The only thing I have to be vigilant about is my grades." It had been a long, long time since Lao Lao was in middle school, so she'd probably forgotten the stress of trying to get good grades. Well, I and any other kid at Groton Middle School could tell you it was pretty dang stressful. I had homework in every class, plus two tests tomorrow. On top of that, I had to practice piano for my recital. The school year had barely begun, and sixth grade was already kicking my butt.

"Winnie, who are you talking to?" came Lisa's huffy voice from the top of the stairs.

Oops. I pressed my finger to my lips, motioning for Lao Lao to stop speaking. With everything that had been going on between my shaman-ing and school, it had slipped my mind to speak quietly to my grandmother around Lisa, who was totally in the dark about the truth of what was going on. And that was how things had to be. The spirit world and human world, kept as separate as possible.

"N-nobody," I called, glancing up at Lisa. She stood at the top of the stairs, crossing her arms over her chest. She blew a huge bubble with her chewing gum and then popped it.

"Talking to yourself." Lisa shook her head. "Why am I not surprised? You're so weird."

"What's it to you?" I snapped. I'd saved my sister's sorry butt yesterday, and here she was being her bossy, snotty self again. Granted, she didn't remember that I'd saved her life yesterday, but still. *I* remembered. Just like how I remembered that Lisa and I used to be best friends, once upon a time. Apparently that little fact had been wiped from my sister's memories, too.

Lesson learned. Next time the evil spirits attacked, I was just going to let them clobber Lisa.

My sister sighed, shaking her head. "Talk to whoever you want—just don't forget to play the piano. And be quieter about it, will you? I have a practice SAT this weekend, and I can't study with all that racket you're always making." Then she flounced back toward her room.

I stuck my tongue out at Lisa's retreating back, and then her door slammed shut.

"Well, you heard Lisa. I gotta practice piano," I said to Lao Lao, shrugging like I was helpless. For once, I did actually feel motivated to play. My next piano recital was coming up later this month, and David would be playing in it, too. I planned to show everyone, once and for all, that *I* was the better piano player.

I sat down on the hard black Vivace bench, placed my fingers on the cool keys, and started playing the opening to Beethoven's Minuet in G, another piece I'd been learning. No sooner had I finished the first stanza than Lao Lao swooped over me again.

"We have to train today, Winnie," insisted Lao Lao. "This is a matter of life and death! You can play piano afterward. First things first—it's time to make mooncakes."

"Again?"

"Until you advance to combining with me, the mooncakes will be your primary source of power."

I could tell I wasn't going to get anything done until I did something to satisfy my nagging grandmother. Sighing, I resigned myself to the task of baking more mooncakes and possibly being attacked by more spirits. So much for avoiding the kitchen for the rest of my life. I couldn't even avoid it for the rest of the week.

Making sure to be as quiet as possible, I grabbed all the ingredients and Lao Lao's cookbook. This time, making the mooncakes wasn't nearly as fun. It wasn't just about creating something yummy for the school bake sale. Now I had to get everything *perfect*. There was the added pressure of Lao Lao correcting me every time I measured out an ingredient wrong.

"No, you're adding too much vegetable oil!" Lao Lao squeaked, causing me to spill vegetable oil all over the counter.

When I'd cleaned up the mess and the batch of moon-cakes was done baking, I stared at the burned desserts on my baking sheet.

"Wrong, wrong, wrong!" tutted my grandmother. "You'll have to try again, Winnie. These mooncakes are no good. You can do better than this."

You can do better than this. Mama and Baba always said those words to me, too. Whenever I brought home an assignment that was less than perfect. Whenever I missed even a single note while playing a piano piece.

"Maybe *I'm* the one who's no good," I muttered under my breath.

"What?"

"Nothing," I said in a louder voice. But that wasn't what I was thinking. What I was thinking was that if I had to spend so much time capturing evil spirits, David was going to beat me in American school, Chinese school, and piano—again. What I was thinking was that stupid David would probably make a better shaman than me in the first place.

"Winnie, careful!"

Too late. Lost in my unpleasant thoughts, I hadn't noticed that my finger was dangerously close to the baking tray—and when I accidentally touched it, the piping-hot pan scalded my skin. "Ow!" Biting my cheeks to keep from crying, I ran to the sink and turned on the cold water, placing my burned finger directly beneath it.

"Are you all right?" My grandmother floated up from behind me, her voice softer with concern. On the counter, Jade had perked up her ears, as if she, too, sensed my distress.

Great. I was such a mess, even my rabbit had to worry about me. Some shaman I was. Forget failing at being a shaman. I was even failing at being the granddaughter of a great chef.

"I'll be fine, Lao Lao," I mumbled. When I removed my finger from the water, I saw that the area of skin where I'd touched the burning-hot baking tray had turned red.

"Here, Winnie, let me wrap it for you—" Lao Lao reached toward me and then stopped. A sad expression crossed her face, as though she'd just remembered she was no longer solid, as she'd been in life. "I can't help you patch up your burn," my grandmother said sadly. "I can only hand items to you that are already on me, like a pamphlet, but not use non-magical items in the human world."

"It's okay. I've got it." I grabbed a Band-Aid from the

handy box we kept next to the sink and wrapped it around my finger. For a moment, my grandmother and I stared at the Band-Aid.

"Try eating a mooncake. Let's see if some good comes out of this batch," said Lao Lao.

Though my finger was still stinging, I obeyed. Carefully, I plucked one of the closest mooncakes out of the tray and bit into it. It was still hot, so I ate it slowly, savoring the way the crust melted in my mouth. I'd burned myself baking this batch of mooncakes, but at least they were pretty darn tasty. They weren't the prettiest mooncakes, but they had to be good for something.

"Now, as a shaman, your ultimate goal is to be able to harness *my* power as your own," said Lao Lao. "Separately, you and I can't do much. But together, we'll be unstoppable." My grandmother beamed at me.

I swallowed a mouthful of the cake before asking, "How am I supposed to channel your power?"

"Close your eyes and empty your mind, Winnie." When I did as she'd instructed, Lao Lao said, "Do you feel the warmth of the mooncake in your belly?"

"Yes."

"Good. Now think of your happiest memories, and try to channel that emotion."

I thought about my first time trying sushi. I thought about how I won the fourth-grade spelling bee two years ago. I thought about lazy days spent at the Suntreader reading manga with Lisa.

As the memories swirled in my mind, something strange happened. My body grew warmer, and then even warmer as I sensed another presence merging with me—Lao Lao's spirit. My palms heated, and I watched with astonishment as the transparent spirit of my grandmother overlapped with my body.

"Whoa. Am I doing it?" I said.

"That's certainly the right idea," said Lao Lao encouragingly.

Then: "WINNIE! DID YOU LEAVE YOUR HAIR IN THE SHOWER DRAIN?"

Lisa's bellow from upstairs shattered my concentration. Just like that, Lao Lao's spirit fled my body. As it did, I felt as though my own spirit had left my body in the process, leaving me exhausted and drained.

"No, I didn't," I protested, not that my sister was listening to me.

"GROSS! DON'T DO IT AGAIN! I ALMOST BARFED JUST NOW," came Lisa's answering shout. A door slammed upstairs, and moments later the shower began running.

Lao Lao had rolled her eyes all the way up to the ceiling, which was a good representation of how I felt.

"I think we can stop here for the day," my grandmother said, her voice trembling. It took me a moment to realize that the trembling was from exhaustion. Not only had joining forces wiped me out, but it appeared to have drained my grandmother's energy, too. "That was a good first attempt.

Now we both need rest. Having proper rest is an important part of the training."

I definitely had the resting part down. I could sleep twelve hours on a good weekend day. "So a shaman and spirit combining forces takes a lot of physical effort?" I said.

Lao Lao nodded gravely. "Yes, but the process of combining does get easier with practice," she said with a reassuring smile.

Practice. Oh brother. I'd never been good at sports or anything physical—in fact, PE was the only subject where I didn't excel—and now I'd gotten saddled with shaman training. This was almost as bad as doing those physical tests in gym class.

"I don't understand why *I'm* the shaman," I mumbled. "Why not Lisa? Lisa's actually good at physical stuff. She even plays softball!"

My grandmother shot me a disapproving look. "I'm not wrong, Winnie. The shaman is *you*. You already fought off the spirit the first time. You're the one who summoned me! You're just like those—those heroes you watch all the time, like that *Sailor Mooncake* show."

"*Sailor Moon,*" I corrected automatically.

"Yes, that. Don't you want to take down rogue spirits and join the Shaman Task Force? Don't you want to be a hero, too?"

A hero. It sounded cool, and honestly, way cooler than my current life. But if I ignored my other duties to dedicate myself to shaman training, how was I ever going to make my family happy? Mama and Baba wouldn't be pleased if they knew I was training to be part of a heroic shaman squad, that was for sure. They'd ask why I hadn't used that time to study harder or practice more piano.

There wasn't anything heroic or special about Winnie Zeng. However I'd stumbled upon my powers, it had to have been a mistake.

I just hoped that, with evil spirits on the loose in the human world, other people wouldn't have to pay the price.

CHAPTER EIGHT

Despite what I'd said to my grandmother, my curiosity about shamanism wouldn't let me rest. Not even at school. I mean, wouldn't you want to learn everything you could if the spirit of your dead grandmother said you were a shaman?

The next day, Mrs. Lee took us to the school library to research mythologies. I took the chance to spend the entire hour looking up articles about the Mid-Autumn Festival, since it was coming up, and Lao Lao had said that spirits would grow in power around the holiday. That research brought me to articles about Hou Yi. Since the legend of Hou Yi was part of Chinese mythology, I was technically doing classwork, even though I wasn't sure yet whether I wanted to do my project on Chinese mythology.

"I'm definitely going to do Greek mythology," I heard Tracy say to her neighbor a few computers down. "It's the *coolest* mythology. I love the story of Persephone and Hades."

Greek mythology. Yeah, it was really cool. We'd focused on learning Greek mythology last year, and I'd read the Percy Jackson series from cover to cover, so I knew way more about Greek mythology than any other mythology, including Chinese. It would be so much easier to do my report on a legend from Greek mythology. People probably expected me to research Chinese mythology anyway.

"You're doing your presentation on Chinese mythology, too?" asked David. He was sitting next to me, unfortunately. We were sitting in alphabetical order, and *Zuo* came right after *Zeng*. This, I realized, was going to become a real problem for me now that David and I went to the same school. I might even have to change my last name.

"I'm not sure yet," I said.

"Chinese legends are so dope." David's eyes lit up. "Oh, the legend of Hou Yi is a really cool one. My mom always told me . . ."

I gave no sign that I wanted to hear more, but that didn't discourage David from launching into a mini-lecture.

According to Google, as well as the Many Annoying Facts David Kept Spouting over My Shoulder Even Though I Never Asked Him, Hou Yi was a powerful archer in Chinese mythology. He was an epic warrior, and I do mean *epic*. Like, Superman probably had nothing on this guy.

Hou Yi was married to this beautiful lady named Chang E, whom he saved from a river monster. Back then, Earth was a miserable place because there were ten suns. Imagine the hottest summer of your life. Now times that by ten. And subtract all the ice cream.

Anyway, Hou Yi must've gotten fed up with living in the scorching heat—possibly, the hot weather made it hard for him to show off his fashionable fall cardigans. (That was, without argument, the worst part of summer.) So he decided to shoot down all the suns at once.

". . . he shot down all but one of the suns," David was saying, still peering at my computer screen. "We learned this story in Chinese school last year, Winnie. Remember?"

"Yeah, of course," I lied. Leave it to David to actually remember stuff from our lessons *last* year. Why couldn't he be normal like the rest of us, and forget all the information he'd memorized as soon as our tests were over?

The only thing I remembered about the legend of Hou Yi and the ten suns was that it was associated with the Mid-Autumn Festival, a.k.a. the one time every year where I was given a ready-made excuse to stuff my face with mooncakes.

Unable to help myself, I snuck a glance over at David's computer screen, just to see what he was looking up. The browser was open to a page about the Mid-Autumn Festival as well.

"Looks like we had the same idea," David said.

"You copied me!" I burst out.

He rolled his eyes. "I didn't *copy* you. I have to learn all this mythology because I have a vested interest in—" His eyes widened, and he shut his mouth, as though he'd almost let something slip that he shouldn't. "Uh . . . because . . . because the Mid-Autumn Festival is around the corner," David said after a beat. "We'll be learning all about it in Chinese school anyway, so I might as well do my presentation on this legend, you know? Kill two birds with one stone."

I narrowed my eyes. Even though he was acting suspicious, David's words made perfect sense. Somehow, the fact that we were on the same wavelength made my project idea seem much less appealing.

"Whatever. Take the easy way out," I sniffed. "I totally wasn't planning to do my presentation on Chinese mythology, anyway. I'm—I'm gonna do Greek mythology."

"Oh yeah? Why are you looking up Chinese legends, then?" David challenged.

"Because I—" *Because I'm trying to figure out more about an evil spirit that's on the loose somewhere in this town.* If I said that, David would collapse out of his seat with laughter. "Oh, what's it to you? Mind your own business."

"I was just asking. Sheesh." He narrowed his eyes at me. I didn't like that searching look on his face. It told me he was about to ask a prying question. "Not to pry, Winnie—"

"Please don't."

David's scowl deepened. "You didn't even let me finish what I was saying."

"That was the point."

"Winnie. David." The sound of Mrs. Lee's sugary-sweet yet tense voice caused David and me to jolt in our seats. The scent of her cinnamon and vanilla perfume wafted toward my nose, and without turning around, I knew she was right behind me. "Is there a problem?"

"Nope," David and I chorused.

"Good. Less talking, more learning," Mrs. Lee said

crisply. Then, after another moment, she moved away, and David and I glared at each other behind her back.

At least Mrs. Lee got our names right this time, I thought. The bar was truly on the floor.

That afternoon, Lisa was away at her SAT prep class, so I had the whole house to myself. Or at least I would have, if it weren't for Lao Lao currently living here rent-free, without anyone else even knowing about it. My grandmother was the definition of a freeloader. Since I didn't yet know how to combine with Lao Lao, she was forced to stay anchored in the body of unsuspecting Jade, who had become the vessel that my grandmother communicated through. The rabbit didn't seem to have a clue what was going on. I envied that.

"Lao Lao, if you're going to sulk in the corner, at least do it quietly," I said. My grandmother had been hovering in the corner of my room right next to my bookshelf, heaving loud sighs every thirty seconds to remind me that she was there.

"We have to train," Lao Lao insisted. "There's no time to waste. Look at you—do you think you have the ability to capture a rogue spirit?"

Ignoring the jab, I checked the clock on my computer and then the planner on my desk, where I'd already written out my whole schedule for the week with a pink gel pen. "Shaman training isn't until four," I informed my grandmother. "Right now it's only three-thirty."

"Ridiculous! Spirits don't operate according to your schedule!"

I put my pencil down, sighing. There was no way I could concentrate on my math homework—not with Lao Lao hovering around me like this. I got up and started to stretch, wincing when my knees cracked in protest. "Fine, then. What's on the training agenda today?"

My grandmother tapped her head. "Mental training."

"Mental training?" I'd been hoping for something cooler, like learning spin kicks.

"Becoming a better shaman relies primarily on strengthening your mental capabilities," said Lao Lao. "Of course, you need to stay in good physical shape as well, but only with a strong mind can you combine with a spirit." She shot me a meaningful look.

That made sense, even if it did sound more exhausting than an algebra set. On the bright side, that meant I didn't have to keep stretching. I sat back down immediately.

"You need to conjure happy feelings," said Lao Lao. "That's why after you ate the mooncakes from my special recipe, you unlocked your powers. Food makes you happy, doesn't it?"

"Yeah." Food made me *ridiculously* happy.

"Now you need to learn how to control that happy feeling. Let it fill your entire body, and open your mind. When your mind is truly open, you'll be able to access my powers. We'll become one in your mind, and you'll be powerful enough to capture even the most chaotic spirits. Does that make sense?"

I nodded. Lao Lao's instructions sounded simple, but I had enough experience with grown-ups to know that whenever they made something sound simple, it was probably going to be anything but.

"Now let's begin," said my grandmother. "Close your eyes and try to channel your happiest memories."

I obeyed. My mind jumped immediately to eating mooncakes. Then it jumped to the memory of the last time I'd spent a whole Saturday at the Suntreader, carefully selecting a new book to spend my precious money on.

Something was working, because I could feel my insides growing warmer, and Lao Lao's voice seemed to be echoing inside my head now. Then, inexplicably, I remembered how David had wiped the floor with me at our last piano competition, and instantly that warm feeling evaporated.

"David!" I groaned.

"Winnie!" shouted my grandmother. "You lost focus. You need to concentrate. You lack discipline!"

I scowled. Leave it to David to mess things up for me when he wasn't even around. We tried again, but it still didn't quite work, probably because right as I started to feel that warm shifting inside me again, intrusive thoughts of my unfinished math homework broke my concentration.

"Never mind," sighed my grandmother, though she

couldn't quite conceal her disappointment. "When I was a young shaman, it took me a while to master the art of combining, too."

"How long?" I asked.

"Hmm . . ." She counted on her fingers. "Twelve hours."

I gaped. "Twelve hours? Lao Lao, you were a prodigy." Well, I had already missed that mark by a long shot. Just half an hour of mental training had thoroughly drained me.

"You need to get some rest now. We'll try again tomorrow," Lao Lao said briskly.

Not only had Lao Lao been a culinary prodigy, but she'd also been a talented shaman. Meanwhile, my abilities couldn't compare in either department. My heart sank. Mostly so we could both stop thinking about the fact that I was so far not acing shaman training, I changed the subject. "Are you sure we need to be training this hard?" I asked. "There's been no sign of anything weird happening in Groton. I mean, besides the usual weird business."

"Evil won't wait for you to strike, Winnie," Lao Lao insisted. "If you think that way, you'll never receive the Spirit Council's approval to be part of the Shaman Task Force."

"What exactly does the Spirit Council do?" I asked.

"Oh, I didn't explain that already?" Lao Lao blinked at me. When I shook my head, she continued, "Forgive your grandmother. My memory grows fuzzier the longer I'm away from the spirit world. I'll be back to normal once I return," she reassured me upon seeing the concern on my face. "The Spirit Council is the council that's in charge of keeping the peace between your world and the spirit realm. It overlooks shamans and tracks the spirits that enter and leave the realm. It goes without saying, of course, that the class one spirit was *not* supposed to be able to escape into this world. The Spirit Council also decides who gets to be part of the Shaman Task Force."

"So are they sort of like the Groton City Council?" That was the only council I'd ever heard of. I didn't know what they did, except sit around a table with little microphones in front of them.

My grandmother frowned. "No, the Spirit Council actually gets work done. Now—enough chitchat. Let's continue your training, but for your body this time. I want to see some stretches."

A few days came and went, and there was still no sign of any malicious spirits stirring in Groton. Nor had I had time to continue training, much to Lao Lao's dismay.

I mean, could my grandmother blame me, though? I had so much on my plate already. Besides a mountain of work at school, including Mrs. Lee's mythology presentation, I had to practice for my upcoming piano recital, which I barely had time to do because I was busy cramming for the Chinese school speech contest. Try saying *that* five times fast.

Though I was normally on top of my game when it came to schoolwork, lately I'd been having trouble keeping up with my obligations, between piano and shaman training. Now I'd fallen way behind. I'd almost forgotten about the speech contest. I was in panic mode, trying to write a three-minute speech about this month's topic—Chinese cuisine—and memorize it.

On the bright side, this time I had a secret weapon to help speed up the process: my grandmother. On the not-so-bright side, Lao Lao's knowledge of Chinese cuisine was over fifty years behind. Also, she wouldn't correct my spelling and grammar for me when I asked, insisting that I do my own work, which I thought was rude.

I quickly learned that if I read the mistakes out loud, though, my grandmother would get so irritated that she'd correct my grammar errors anyway.

It was the most stressful week of my life, but somehow, by late Saturday night, just twelve hours before the contest began, I'd managed to pull it off. I had a whole speech prepared and memorized. And I was totally going to knock the pants off my competition.

If I won, maybe my parents would let me slow down, just for a bit. Maybe they'd be happy and proud of me. That was more important to me than anything else in my life, including shaman training. Sorry, Lao Lao.

As I headed for bed the night before the speech contest, my grandmother harrumphed over in the corner of the room. I looked up at her and frowned.

"I told you, I just have to take care of this Chinese speech contest first," I said, rubbing my eyes sleepily. "After that, I can do more mental training or whatever."

"By then, it may be too late," Lao Lao snapped. "We might be under another attack!"

Now I saw where Lisa got her dramatics from. My grandmother had clearly passed along that gene. "Look, I've got a lot going on right now, okay?" I burst out. "Mama and Baba have super high expectations of me, and I can't let them down. We'll have to train another time."

Lao Lao sniffed but didn't reply. I flipped off the light and then turned onto my side, burrowing into my blankets in the darkness.

"Good night, Lao Lao."

I thought I heard my grandmother reply, but within moments, I was fast asleep.

The next morning, I was awoken by pounding on my door, and the rare sound of my father's voice yelling at me.

"WINNIE, GET UP! WE'RE GOING TO BE LATE!"

Still blinking sleep out of my eyes, I reached over and fumbled for my phone to check the time. It was 8:20 a.m. Oh no. The Chinese speech contest was supposed to start at nine a.m. sharp, and my Chinese school was a forty-minute drive away. I'd have to leave at this exact moment if I wanted to get there on time.

I shot out of bed, thankful that I'd laid out my outfit the day before, a purple blazer paired with purple dress pants. Wearing the outfit made me look much more put together than I felt.

As I scrambled to brush through the tangles in my hair, Lao Lao almost gave me a heart attack by swooping in front of me. I dropped my hairbrush in shock. "Ack! Lao Lao, don't *do* that!"

"Take me to your Chinese school," my grandmother ordered.

"What? Why do you wanna come along? *I* don't even wanna go." If middle school was the armpit of the education system, then Chinese school was . . . whatever was smellier than an armpit. Toe jam, maybe. Chinese school was the toe jam of the education system.

"I haven't left the house yet, Winnie," Lao Lao huffed.

"So leave, then. I'm not stopping you."

"I can't. Not on my own. I'm not strong enough to go around without being anchored to your rabbit, since it was the vessel I was transported to this world in. Will you really let your poor grandmother stay cooped up in here forever?"

"Yes, because I can't carry a rabbit around everywhere with me. How would that look?" It really must have been a long time since Lao Lao had gone to school. Possibly back in her day, rabbits were free to roam middle schools.

"If you ask me, you care a little too much about your appearance," my grandmother said. "If you never take me around town, how am I supposed to help you track down the evil spirits?"

I sighed. I was running late, Baba was yelling again, and I was trying to remember my Chinese speech. It was a wonder my head didn't explode. "All right, *all right*. You can come along," I finally said in exasperation.

I scooped up Jade from the floor and thought quickly. How was I supposed to hide a whole rabbit from my family and everyone at Chinese school? I grabbed Jade's portable cage from the foot of my bed, placed her inside, and shoved the cage into my Pusheen backpack. Good thing this bag was huge. I zipped the bag up three-quarters of the way so my pet rabbit could breathe.

"Okay. You can come with me, but on one condition," I told Lao Lao, raising a stern finger. In the back of my mind, I could vaguely appreciate the absurdity of the situation, where somehow *I* was the one laying down the law to my grandmother instead of the other way around. "You absolutely, definitely, *cannot* talk to me. Especially not when I'm giving my speech." I paused. "Well, unless it's a total emergency. Like, building-on-fire, evil-spirit-destroying-Earth kind of emergency. Promise?"

My grandmother pursed her lips, then slowly nodded. "Promise. And don't forget to bring your mooncakes, and a jar just in case we have to capture a rogue spirit."

I grabbed a ziplock bag of mooncakes off my desk, leaving one more bag behind for another emergency. Then I took a mason jar from the top of my dresser and put it into my backpack, which was full to bursting by now. Better to be safe than sorry. After grabbing my backpack, I flung open my bedroom door and took the stairs down two at a time.

Dang, I really hoped I wouldn't regret bringing my pet rabbit and the spirit of my shaman grandmother to Chinese school.

CHAPTER NINE

If I thought I'd be able to get peace and quiet during the car ride, I was sorely mistaken. Lao Lao kept her promise not to talk to me, but unfortunately my living relatives had made no such promise. On the contrary, they seemed determined to be as loud and disruptive as possible. Mama had to run errands today, so Baba drove us to Chinese school. And, well, my father being a lawyer and all, he just couldn't resist arguing up a storm—with his teenage daughter.

"Lisa, since when did you start wearing makeup? That blue color on your eyes is too much. You should take it off," my father barked.

"I've been wearing makeup for almost a year now. You might've noticed sooner if you were ever home," Lisa quipped. "And I'll wear whatever color eye shadow I like. I'm not doing it for *your* approval."

"Winnie doesn't wear makeup. You shouldn't, either."

"Winnie and I are *different people*. Don't compare us," my sister said. Her tone of voice in saying *different people* suggested she hated us being lumped together. I wasn't sure if I was hurt by that, or if I agreed. Lisa and I *were* different people. I hated when our parents pitted us against each other.

I stifled a groan and hunched over, hoping to slink through the car seat. I hated whenever Lisa and Baba fought—which was a lot, ever since Lisa had discovered the art of back talk. Today, though, their arguing was worse than usual. I attributed it to the abnormally gross weather. Nobody seemed to be in a good mood, including me. I really couldn't wait to get Chinese school over with today.

"Since you started high school, you think you can talk back to me?" Baba snapped. "I could turn this car around right now."

"Do it," Lisa challenged. "You'd be doing me a favor. Chinese school is such a waste of time."

Even for Lisa, this back talk was a bit much. Both my father and sister seemed to be running hotter tempers than usual, in contrast to the stormy, cold fall weather.

"Waste of time? *Waste of time?*" Baba echoed angrily. "Learning your native language is not a waste of—"

"It's not *my* native language. My native language is English. I'm barely Chinese, okay? I've never even been to China!"

Privately, I thought Lisa had a point, but I could also kind of see Baba's point, too. I didn't like Chinese school, but it would feel even worse to know nothing about Chinese.

"That doesn't mean you aren't Chinese—"

"Can you guys please be quieter? I can't focus on my speech," I blurted out when I finally couldn't take it any longer. My eyes were glued to my notebook as I read over my speech, testing myself to make sure I had it memorized. At this point, I had no idea what I did and didn't have memorized anymore. All I could do was make the speech and hope I didn't totally forget everything while I was up there.

Baba let out a breath and then said in a carefully measured way, "Lower your voice, Lisa. Your sister is studying. You should be more like Winnie."

Though I hated to admit it, a small part of me was thrilled to hear Baba praise me, even if he was once again comparing us, this time at Lisa's cost. At least it meant my father thought I was doing something right.

But Baba's words added pressure, too. No doubt he'd expect me to keep up the good work.

For a moment, Lisa looked like she wanted to retort. Then she rolled her eyes and clamped her mouth shut. She shot me a glare, like it was my fault she and Baba had been fighting.

"What?" I said.

Lisa stuck her AirPods into her ears and ignored us for the rest of the drive.

Traffic was mercifully light, which was good, since we were crunched for time. A little more than half an hour later, we pulled into the parking lot of Sherman Community College, where New Chapter Chinese School was held every Sunday. A throbbing headache had developed over my left eye. It didn't help my mood that huge gray clouds hung in the sky above, and already a light drizzle had begun.

"There's supposed to be a thunderstorm later today," Baba sighed. "Hopefully, it'll hold off until school is over."

One glance at the car's digital clock up front told me that it was 9:07 a.m. Which meant the speech contest had officially started seven minutes ago. Which meant I was screwed.

I prayed that this event was running late, like most Chinese school events did. I shoved my notebook into my backpack, careful to place it on top of Jade's cage.

"See you later!" I yelled. Without waiting for a response, I sprinted for the front entrance.

Room 204. That was where the Chinese speech contest was being held. It took me several precious moments to find the classroom on the college building's giant directory, and several more to navigate my way down the halls to find the right room.

I burst into the classroom just in time to see a tall, short-haired girl walk to the podium up front.

At least thirty pairs of eyes, belonging to a mix of judges and contestants, turned toward me. My face burned with embarrassment. I hunched my shoulders, trying to make myself as small as possible as I speed-walked over to a stern-looking lady with her black hair swept up in a tight bun. Principal Tang. She was sitting behind a desk with a piece of cardboard taped to it that read SIGN-INS.

As soon as my eyes met the principal's intimidating gaze, an eerie, cold sensation settled in my chest. But then a moment later, it was gone.

I shook my head to clear it. My nerves were really getting to me. "Hi," I said. "Um, my name is—"

"Zeng Weini?" interrupted Principal Tang.

"Yeah. Zeng Weini from Class 6B. I'm here for the speech contest," I added unnecessarily.

"You're just in time." The disapproving look on the principal's face told me that I should've been there way earlier. "You're up next. Take this and go sit in one of the empty chairs." Principal Tang handed me a sheet of paper with the number 200 and a piece of tape on it.

Familiar faces gazed out at me from the crowd. I recognized Allison Tan, sitting in the back, who flashed me a weak smile. She sat next to a couple of my classmates, including Dennis Chu and Michael Ho. But all the seats near them were already taken.

I plopped down in the nearest empty seat and did my best to ignore the sneer on David's face across the room. We'd see who was sneering after the Chinese speech contest was over. I planned to out-speech everyone, David included, and show my parents the fruits of all my hard work.

The principal cleared her throat. "Now that we've handled that *rude interruption,* you may begin," she told the contestant at the podium, giving her a nod.

If I'd thought my cheeks were burning before, now they were surely on fire. *Rude interruption.* Great. I'd already left a bad impression on the judges. That meant I'd really have to go out of my way to knock their socks off with my speech.

Speaking of my speech, I only had a few more minutes to cram for it. I'd hoped to be among the last few contestants to go, which would have given me a good chunk of time to keep memorizing, but no such luck.

I dug my notebook out of my backpack and began to read faster than I'd ever read in my life. By the time I'd made it twice through the whole speech, everyone was applauding the speaker before me, and in the commotion, David slipped out of the room.

Uh-oh. Time was up.

Quickly, I stowed my notebook under my chair. I joined in the clapping as the previous girl, flushing, returned to her seat. Lucky girl. I wanted to be the one who was already done with the torture.

"Next up is Zeng Weini from Class 6B," announced the principal.

I stood up so fast that I almost tripped over my own feet, causing a couple of younger kids to snicker. Great. It was going to take a miracle for me to finish this speech without fatally embarrassing myself and all my ancestors.

No, don't think like that, Winnie. You've been practicing so hard all week. You've just gotta be confident.

Confident. Ha. Easier said than done.

I took my place behind the podium and breathed in and out before looking up at the crowd of contestants and judges. The spirit of my grandmother hovered over the seat I'd just vacated, and she gave me two big thumbs up. Somehow, the sight of Lao Lao managed to calm my racing heart, just a little. I smiled, nodded, and opened my mouth to begin my speech.

All worries of shamanism and school flew out of my head. For a few minutes, my mind was blissfully empty of everything except the speech I'd memorized. All my practice had paid off, because my mouth already knew the right words. They came pouring out.

With just the last fifteen seconds of my speech left to go, a sense of accomplishment filled me. Why had I gotten so worked up earlier? I had this thing in the bag. The speech contest had been a total cinch. *First prize, here I come.*

Then lightning flashed bright white outside, interrupting the flow of my speech. I lost my train of thought. The lightning was followed by a huge clap of thunder, so close that it shook the whole building.

As everyone gasped, the lights in the classroom flickered off. A second later, they flickered on. By then I'd been startled out of my intense concentration.

"Um . . . where was I?" I said. It was no use. I'd lost the audience's attention.

A loud crash echoed in the room.

"What was that?" a girl yelled.

"AGGGGGGGHHHHHHHHHHHH! THERE'S A GIANT RAT!" shrieked Principal Tang, leaping up onto her seat and crouching in terror. She pointed toward the empty seat I'd vacated. "A *rat*. I want it out!"

If I hadn't been so stunned, the sight of our principal totally losing it might've been funny. But what happened next was most definitely *not* funny.

More crashing noises ensued. A small metal cage tumbled out of my backpack. The metal door flung wide open, and a white fur ball shot out of it. The spirit of my grandmother floated above Jade and then whizzed around in a panic.

"Winnie! We have a problem!" cried Lao Lao, as if that weren't obvious. She hovered next to me, flapping her arms around in a panic. "This is an emergency. There's a spirit on the—"

"Not now, Lao Lao!"

"But, Winnie—"

I waved her off. Evil spirits could come later. Right now I had a bigger, furrier problem to handle, in the form of my rabbit, which was streaking around the classroom.

I was really gonna be in for it now.

Everyone began screaming and backing away from Jade, which I thought was a bit of an overreaction. Jade wasn't even a rat!

"Someone catch that rat now!" bellowed Principal Tang. She placed her hand over her heart, looking on the verge of fainting.

In all the chaos, Jade ran much faster than I'd ever seen her go, shooting across the floor and toward the door. I dove after my rabbit, but David, who'd returned to the room without my noticing, got there first. He scooped up Jade and hugged her in his arms, patting her terrified, shaking head.

"David, give her to me—"

"Who brought a rat to school?" one of the other teachers shrieked.

"She's not a rat. She's my *rabbit*!" I shouted without thinking. Oops. I realized my mistake the moment everyone turned their accusing eyes to me.

"Zeng Weini." Principal Tang raised a shaking finger at me, her eyes narrowed with cold fury. Once again, that cold sensation gripped me—this time, I was pretty sure it was dread of the punishment that awaited me. "My office. Now."

Oh boy. Now I'd really done it.

CHAPTER TEN

One thing you should know about me is that I never, ever get in trouble. And I mean never, ever, ever. *Never*. Winnie Zeng doesn't do bad things.

I guess it would be more accurate to say that the *old* Winnie Zeng didn't do bad things. Because sneaking a rabbit into a classroom, despite knowing that the New Chapter Chinese School had a strict policy against pets, was not a *good* thing.

I was just lucky nobody knew Lao Lao was here, too. I didn't know where "spirits of grandmothers" ranked on the Chinese school's list of Banned Classroom Items, but it was probably pretty high.

My grandmother floated above my shoulder, waving her arms around as she spoke to me, but I wasn't listening. Even if Jade's escape from my backpack wasn't Lao Lao's fault, the fact that I'd had to sneak Jade into the classroom in the first place *was* her fault. I didn't feel like talking to her at *all*.

My ears rang with Principal Tang's harsh words. Uh-oh. I'd never gotten in trouble at school before. Ever. Unlike Lisa, who used to have some behavior problems before she started softball, I'd always made sure to follow the rules. Mama and Baba would be so upset if they found out. *I* was upset that this had happened.

"What on earth were you thinking?" snapped Principal Tang when we entered her office. I was in front of the armchair, while the principal stood cross-armed in front of her desk. She appeared to have mostly recovered from the shock of Jade's great escape. The only remaining evidence of her major freak-out session were the strands of hair that had fallen loose from her tight bun, and her slightly pink cheeks. And her eyes, which remained as cold as ever. "Bringing a rat to school!"

"Rabbit," I corrected automatically.

Bad move. That only made the principal puff up her cheeks in anger. She resembled a chipmunk, but I decided now was not the time to point that out. "Rat, rabbit, whatever! I don't care. The point is, you've broken school rules, and you'll face the consequences. You're disqualified from the Chinese speech contest."

I hung my head. Shame burned through me at Principal Tang's words. Even though I wanted to protest—I mean, I'd worked *so* hard on that speech—part of me knew that I deserved what I got. After all, I was the one who'd knowingly broken the rules. Even if it was for Lao Lao. Even if it was for the greater good, or whatever my grandmother would tell me later.

Well, now that I was in the hot seat, all I could say was that the greater good had *not* been worth it. I didn't feel like a hero working toward the greater good. I felt like the horrible, awful, no-good villain, especially with Principal Tang glaring down at me like that. My chest tightened. My insides turned icy. Sweat made my palms slick.

"Winnie, you need to get out of here right now," Lao Lao insisted. "You—"

I was too upset with my grandmother to listen to her, so I shook my head and tried to drown out her voice. Didn't she see that this was *so* not the time to worry about hunting evil spirits? I was currently in the most perilous situation of my life.

Just when I thought things couldn't get worse, the door swung open. The last person I wanted to see stepped through the doorway.

"I've got the rabbit," David said, holding up Jade in his arms. "And your stuff, Winnie." He turned around to show that he was wearing both his black backpack and my Pusheen backpack. There was an awkward look on his face, like he knew he was interrupting a bad scene, which made me even more ashamed. I didn't need sympathy from David.

"Very good, Dawei," said Principal Tang, her nostrils flaring. She spared him a glance, nodding almost imperceptibly, before turning her glare back to me. "As I was saying, we'll need to discuss punishment for your little prank, young lady."

As I squirmed under the principal's glower, David shut the door.

"Thanks, David," I muttered, holding out my arms for Jade.

But Principal Tang intervened swiftly, placing her arm between us to block David from getting any closer. "Not so fast," the principal snarled. Her piercing eyes were narrowed in fury as she puffed out her chest.

Rain pelted the window outside. Principal Tang drew herself to her full height. She grew taller.

And taller.

And taller.

And *taller.*

To top it all off, her angry eyes began flashing red. At the same time, the lights in the room flickered. Lightning flashed outside, accompanied seconds later by a clap of thunder.

Okay, I was no expert, but I was pretty sure this was not normal Chinese school principal behavior. Things had officially gone from bad to freaky.

I stumbled backward, gawking at her growing form. The principal was scary on a regular basis, but this was over-the-top even for her. She'd doubled—no, tripled—in size. Her eyes glowed a threatening red, and her skin had turned dark green. Her mouth had become a snarl, and her teeth had grown into sharp white fangs. We were definitely dealing with someone—or *something*—otherworldly. It took every last shred of my resolve not to turn around and run screaming in the opposite direction.

"That's what I warned you about," shouted Lao Lao. "Your principal has been possessed by a class two spirit. Oh, these spirits are getting clever—I didn't sense it until it was too late!"

A class two spirit. Oh no. I'd had a hard enough time against the class one spirit the other day.

"This is very strange," my grandmother shouted.

She could say that again. "You're telling me! We're being attacked by a spirit at Chinese school!"

"No, I mean—class two spirits, like class one spirits, aren't usually smart enough to target shamans on their own. It's almost like . . . this one was sent here to target you both, like the class one spirit, by an even more powerful spirit." As Lao Lao spoke, her eyes widened, and she turned a fearful gaze toward David and me.

I had no idea what my grandmother was talking about, nor could I spare much thought for it. First we had to deal with the matter of my Chinese school principal being possessed by a class two spirit.

"Um . . . P-P-Principal Tang?" David stammered.

Principal Tang cackled and raised her hands. Random bits of school supplies, like pencils and scissors, levitated off the desk and began zooming around the room.

"Rude!" David dodged a large pink eraser that whizzed by his ear.

"Winnie, what are you standing there for?" Lao Lao yelled. "Use your powers!"

Though I knew my grandmother was right, I couldn't move. My legs were frozen, feet rooted to the spot. A million thoughts were racing through my mind, but one rose to the fore—the fact that poor David was getting caught in the cross fire of a supernatural battle that he was definitely *not* equipped for.

"David, get out of here!" I shouted, turning around.

But David wasn't running. David was reaching down to unzip his backpack. He pulled something green and scaly out of it, something that *moved*.

"SNAKE!" I screamed.

"He's an iguana! His name is Qianlong. Named after the one and only Emperor Qianlong," David said, frowning at me. "Show some respect, Winnie."

Before I could even process what was happening, a silvery ghost rose out of the iguana in David's hand. It was the figure of an old man with a waist-length beard. He wore fancy, swooshy red-and-gold robes embellished with colorful dragons. On his head sat a gold hat with red tassels, and his white hair was braided down his back.

My jaw dropped. This man looked like a *real* emperor. He could've stepped right off the set of one of those Chinese historical dramas Mama loved so much. If he had been dressed any fancier, C-drama lovers everywhere would have been asking for his autograph. This man was so official-looking, his name was bound to be something equally important-sounding, like Lao Zi or Confucius or—

"Joe!" shouted David, waving at the old man like they were buddies. He dropped his pet iguana onto the desk, where it cowered behind a stapler.

"Joe?" I spluttered.

"That's my American name—don't wear it out," Joe said with a wink.

"Oh, not *you!*" cried my grandmother. She glowered at Joe as though they were mortal enemies and she had half a mind to chase him out right then.

"What the heck is going on?" I shouted, but my question was answered seconds later, when David and the spirit named Joe combined. There was a burst of blue light, and then David was no longer just David. Blue energy enveloped him. I stumbled back, my jaw dropping. When David opened his eyes, they glowed bright white, his pupils vanished. The spirit of the old man hovered over his outline.

"See that? *That's* what it means for a shaman and their overspirit to combine," Lao Lao said unnecessarily. "Take notes, Winnie."

It was impossible, but the undeniable proof was right before my eyes.

David Zuo was a shaman.

CHAPTER ELEVEN

This news might have shocked a different Winnie, but I had reached the point where pretty much nothing could stun me ever again. If the sky fell on me, or if skinny jeans came back into fashion, I would simply accept fate.

My Chinese school principal was possessed by a spirit. David was a shaman. David's overspirit was named . . . Joe. Yeah, sixth grade was being totally normal so far.

I dove toward my backpack, which David had dropped onto the floor in all the mayhem. Sidestepping a notebook that had zoomed toward my foot, I yanked my ziplock bag of mooncakes out of the backpack. Since I hadn't yet mastered the art of combining, I was going to have to resort to pelting Principal Tang with a bunch of magical baked goods and hope that did the job.

David and the principal were already locked in combat. Blue jets of light shot out of David's palms, but Principal Tang was able to dodge them easily, and instead they hit the wall and knocked over a bookshelf. The principal was gaining ground on him, deflecting David's attacks with nothing more than her bare hands.

Lao Lao swooped down and grabbed a handful of mooncakes. She began pelting Principal Tang with them. The mooncakes bounced off the principal's body but left angry red welts on her green skin where they'd hit, causing her to roar with agony. Quickly, I joined my grandmother, picking up the mooncakes she'd thrown, to chuck them again at the spirit. "Take that!"

Rather than shrink back or even show any signs of damage, the possessed principal laughed, though the mooncakes did seem to at least have the effect of slowing down her mayhem. The classroom supplies floated half-heartedly in the air, some of them dropping to the ground, as if they'd just remembered they were bound by the law of gravity.

I bit my lip in frustration. The mooncakes I'd baked weren't magical enough. Weren't good enough. *I* wasn't good enough at being a shaman.

"Winnie, why aren't you doing anything? Move!" My grandmother was still throwing mooncakes at the spirit, but it just batted them away as though they were nothing more than pesky flies.

"I . . . I . . ." *I'm not a hero, Lao Lao. I'm a fraud. And a coward. This is the proof.*

Principal Tang roundhouse-kicked David, sending him flying across the floor. The attack was so strong that it severed the connection between David and the spirit. With a burst of white light, the old man went sailing out the open window, and now David was just David again, huddling on the floor, shaking.

My grandmother had run out of ammo and was backing away as the spirit cornered her. The mooncakes were lying around the principal's desk, out of Lao Lao's reach. And I was rooted to the spot in horror, defenseless.

"You old, interfering fools. Why won't you go peacefully back to the spirit realm and leave me alone?" the class two spirit snarled. "You're dead now—why do you care what happens on Earth?"

"Because I, unlike you, have a conscience," snapped Lao Lao. "Not to mention much nicer hair!"

"It's not *my* fault this stuffy old woman needs a makeover!" shrieked the spirit, tugging at Principal Tang's limp hair.

At once, pride surged through me. Even cornered, my grandmother was still putting up a fight. But I imagined she wouldn't be able to for long. The class two spirit, seemingly so offended by Lao Lao's last comment that it had snapped, moved in on my grandmother, raising its hands and squeezing my grandmother's throat.

"NO!" The scream was ripped from me before I even realized it was mine. My brain quickly processed new information—that humans could apparently harm spirits if they were possessed by another spirit. The sight of Lao Lao struggling in the spirit's grasp jolted me into action.

I didn't hesitate for a second before sprinting across the room and grabbing as many mooncakes as my arms could carry. Then I raced back and began throwing them at the spirit possessing Principal Tang, channeling all my fury into each motion. Everything disappeared except my target, the mooncakes, and the white-hot anger that seared through my chest. Maybe I couldn't combine with Lao Lao yet, and maybe that made me a bad shaman. But I still needed to do the best I could at the moment. "Get away from my grand-mother!"

One by one, the mooncakes hit their mark, striking the back of the spirit's neck and head. It shrieked and released Lao Lao at once, who floated away, rubbing her throat.

As the spirit continued to scream in pain, my eyes wid-ened, and I realized that huge red welts that resembled burn marks had risen where the mooncakes had hit it. Only then did I notice that the mooncakes had turned hot in my hands. But rather than burning me, they felt pleasantly warm, like they were fresh out of the oven.

"Finish it off, Winnie!" David choked out.

Without wasting another moment, I used all my might to throw the last two mooncakes at the spirit. It turned its head at precisely the wrong second. Both mooncakes hit it square in the face at the same moment. The combined ef-fect seemed to do the trick. There was a burst of light and a sizzling noise.

"Oh, that's gonna leave a mark," I said.

The mooncakes fell to the floor, leaving behind a huge red burn on Principal Tang's face. The spirit tottered back-ward, limbs flailing as it tried to steady itself, but there was nothing to grasp but empty air. It fell down and crumpled in a heap.

A moment later, the silvery-white wisp of the spirit rose out of the body of the principal.

"Don't let that spirit escape," shouted Lao Lao. "Get the jar, Winnie. The jar!"

I moved quickly to obey. My grandmother dove wildly through the air with her arms outstretched, as though to catch the evil spirit. The spirit easily outstripped Lao Lao's arms, darting past them—and right into the mason jar I'd pulled out of my backpack. I turned the lid so that the jar was sealed shut.

"Good reflexes," my grandmother complimented me.

Panting, I managed a small smile and stuffed the jar into my backpack. Then I turned to gaze at the mess surrounding us.

The school supplies were strewn all over the floor as if a tornado had swept through. The unconscious principal was lying on the floor. David was collapsed against the principal's desk, holding a notebook over his head, as though he thought that would protect him. He looked nothing like the fearless shaman he'd been moments ago.

Sympathy surged through me at the sight of him cowering there in terror. "David? Are you okay?"

"Do you *think* I'm okay?" he yelled. Then he shook his head and glanced around frantically. "Where did my great-great-great-great-grandfather go?"

"Who?" I said blankly. Then it clicked. "That spirit—Joe—is your relative?"

"Yes. And he was an emperor in his mortal life, so you should address him with more respect," David sniffed. "Call him Emperor Joe."

"I am not doing that," I said. "That's the most ridiculous thing I've ever heard."

David must have privately agreed, because he had no comeback.

This was too much to process. I had to lean against the wall to steady myself as I reeled with the information. Now Joe's manner of dress made sense, but at the same time, everything else made even less sense than before.

"So, let me get this straight." I pressed my fingers to my temple. "You're descended from a freaking *emperor*?"

"Bit slow on the uptake, aren't you?"

Some of my sympathy for David vanished. "Excuse me for not knowing that *you've been a shaman all along.* Excuse me for having no clue that you're descended from an *emperor.*" No wonder David was so insufferable all the time, swaggering around like he was royalty. There was actual royal blood in his veins. And all I knew about my ancestors was that they'd been farmers for generations. No, I could never tell that to David now. He'd laugh himself silly. Even though being a farmer was totally acceptable, anyway. "And it's not like you knew I was a shaman, either!" I pointed out.

"Maybe not," admitted David, "but I did know there was *a* shaman in Groton. Why do you think I willingly transferred from Stuyvale to Groton Middle School? Definitely not for the quality of the education. The Spirit Council assigned Joe and me here to help strengthen the protection in this town. And good thing they did, too." He wrinkled his nose and looked at me with disdain.

Looked like even getting knocked to the floor hadn't taken David down a peg. He was as stuck-up as ever. Rolling my eyes, I strode across the room, grabbed the notebook out of his limp fingers, and bopped David on the head with it.

"Hey! What was that for?"

"Because you're annoying."

David rubbed the top of his head and frowned at me. He muttered something under his breath that sounded awfully like, "*You're* the nuisance."

"So the Spirit Council made you transfer schools," I said. "How do they have the power to do that?"

"They gave Joe a message to pass on to me," David explained. "Technically, I didn't *have* to transfer, because the Spirit Council can't force anyone to do something they don't want to—it's voluntary. But if I refused, then they wouldn't consider me for the Shaman Task Force, so..." He shrugged. "I had to make a tough decision. Even if it meant sacrificing my education."

"Hey, Groton Middle School isn't *that* bad." There was David's private-school snootiness again. Any goodwill I'd mistakenly felt toward him vanished.

Before I could retort, an interruption came in the form of David's overspirit floating back in through the window. He made a beeline not for David but for Lao Lao.

"Hello," said Joe in a frosty voice. "Didn't get a chance to properly greet you before . . . all that happened."

"Hmph." Lao Lao didn't even pretend to be friendly toward the other spirit. She narrowed her eyes. "I see you're as useless as ever, Joe. Falling out of windows now, are we?"

"You're one to talk," retorted Joe. "You couldn't even combine with your shaman. You had to resort to throwing *mooncakes* at your opponent. What is this, a food market fight? That display was just embarrassing."

My grandmother's cheeks darkened, which was the closest a spirit could get to blushing. Great. She *was* embarrassed. And it was my fault, for not being able to combine with her yet. Shame flooded my body from head to toe.

"Oh, you want to talk about embarrassing?" Lao Lao snapped. "Why don't we start with the entirety of your career as an overspirit?"

David and I glanced at each other in confusion, and for a moment I forgot Joe's dig about combining. The air practically crackled with the negative energy between the two spirits. I had a feeling that there was a long, unpleasant history between the two of them.

"Um," I interrupted, "do you two know each other?"

Lao Lao didn't break her stare-down with David's ancestor. "Oh, yes. Joe and I had been working together as shaman recruiters for a while, before we got summoned to be your overspirits."

"We were—are—rivals," clarified Joe. "You were always trying—and *failing*—to capture more rogue spirits than me."

"Ha! Your memory must be going, old man. *I* seem to remember that I captured five hundred and eleven spirits over the course of the last year, whereas you only captured a measly five hundred and nine."

Joe seethed. "I was the five hundred and eleven, you old bat. You were five-oh-nine."

"Oh, the ancient-as-fossils emperor calling *me* old. That's rich!"

"EVERYONE, STOP ARGUING!" David's shout did the job, causing both spirits to startle and turn their attention to him instead. He crossed his arms over his chest and glared. "Can you both explain what the heck is going on here?"

CHAPTER TWELVE

Once the two overspirits had finally stopped yelling at each other—though they continued to glare daggers—we were finally, spirits and shamans alike, able to get on the same page.

I gave David the rundown of what Lao Lao and I had been doing so far, starting from me unleashing her spirit when I was baking mooncakes. David, in turn, explained that he'd come into his sixth sense and developed shaman powers earlier in the summer when he'd turned eleven.

"So you knew all this time that there was another shaman in town, but you didn't know who it was?" I said.

"Yeah, and the Spirit Council didn't give me any pointers, either," David grumbled.

"Most shamans operate alone," Joe informed us. "They don't interact with one another unless it's for a Shaman Task Force meeting, or some other special assignment."

"So why do I have to be stuck with this doofus—I mean, dude?" I said, pointing at David.

"Hey, I heard what you said!"

"Groton has just become a new portal city, so it's easier

for spirits to cross over into the human world," explained Lao Lao. "It requires more heavy guarding. Normally one town only requires the protection of one shaman, but the Spirit Council decided to assign the two of you to Groton, just to be on the safe side."

"It's too bad they couldn't have picked a more capable spirit to help guide Winnie," said Joe, not bothering to whisper.

A vein pulsed in Lao Lao's forehead. "Too bad, isn't it, that for David, they chose an old man who falls out of a window at the slightest sign of trouble."

"That class two spirit was *strong*, and you know it. And— and anyway, it was the wind! I'm better than that," snapped Joe defensively.

I rubbed my head, already feeling the throbbing sensation of an oncoming headache. I had a feeling I was going to be getting a lot of headaches from now on.

David glanced from Lao Lao to me, then back to Lao Lao and back to me again. His jaw had dropped slightly. "I still can't believe the other shaman in town is *you*, Winnie. What are the odds?"

"Well, maybe it's better that you two already know each other," said Lao Lao briskly. "You can team up and protect this town."

"Team up?" David and I said in unison.

I couldn't believe I had to team up with David. There had to be a mistake. Not David. *Anyone* but David. I'd rather team up with Lisa. I'd rather team up with Bigfoot. The last thing I needed was to hang around David even more. As if I didn't already see his face enough at Chinese school *and* American school.

This day was definitely ending up on the Top Ten Worst Hits of Winnie Zeng for sure. Shaking my head, I lowered my gaze to the floor. The scattered mess of school supplies and squashed mooncakes served as undeniable evidence of what had just happened in the principal's office.

David, a shaman. The universe had to be laughing at me. For our whole lives, David and I had constantly been put head-to-head with each other. From taking drawing lessons when we were really young, to learning piano, to attending the same Chinese school, and now going to the same American public school. We were always competing against each other.

It figured that we were both shamans, too. It figured that this sixth sense, the shaman powers that I might've thought were my own, *also* belonged to David Zuo.

"I'm sorry, I—I think I need a moment," David said. He raised a hand to his forehead and rubbed it, as though trying to rid himself of a headache.

An awkward silence fell between us. The kind of awkwardness that happens when you and your archnemesis have just teamed up to take down an evil spirit with a bunch of mooncakes, and when you've both recently learned that you're shamans.

After a few moments, the silence was interrupted by the

sound of something vibrating in my pocket. It took me a moment to realize what it was: my phone. I glanced at the screen to see who was calling me, and my heart thudded. It was Baba.

I picked up his call immediately, because I didn't have a death wish. "Hello?"

"Winnie, where are you? Your sister and I have been waiting in the car for twenty minutes now."

I glanced up at the digital clock on the wall. It was eleven-twenty. Chinese school had ended twenty minutes ago, and I hadn't noticed, thanks to, well, everything that had just happened.

"Shoot. School already ended. I gotta go," I said. Scrambling to my feet, I grabbed my backpack. Jade was sitting on the shelf where David had left her, still out of the way of trouble. I coaxed her back into her cage, returned the cage to the bag, and zipped it three-quarters of the way. My foot caught on something. I glanced down and saw that it was the unconscious principal's sleeve.

"Help me pick up Principal Tang, will you?" I said to David, gesturing toward the principal's motionless body. That had to be the strangest thing I'd ever said while at Chinese school.

David blinked and then shook his head, as though snapping out of a reverie. "Yeah, sure." He grabbed her right arm, while I hooked my arm under Principal Tang's left armpit. Together we heaved her up into a sitting position on the floor behind her desk. I rearranged her hands, placing them on top of each other. Now it looked like she'd dozed off. Hopefully.

David and I stood back to admire our handiwork. Then my phone buzzed again. This time it was a text from Lisa.

> **Lisa:** WHERE THE HECK ARE YOU? HURRY UP AND COME TO THE CAR!!!

Lisa wasn't a particularly polite texter, but the all-caps shouting was atypical even for her. She must've still been in a foul mood. And keeping her waiting was the last thing I wanted to do.

"Um, so, I gotta run," I told David with a weird sort of half shrug. "Um . . . see you at school tomorrow?" Being nice to David felt so strange. So unnatural. Even more unnatural than spirits running amok in Groton.

"Yeah, I'll see you—"

Before either of us could make a move, the door banged open. A tall man and a short lady, who I recognized as the third-grade teachers Mr. Wu and Mrs. Lin, burst into the room. Behind them trailed a small group of students, who were peering into the classroom curiously.

"We heard reports of some loud noises," said Mr. Wu. "Did something happen?" His mouth parted in surprise as his gaze fell upon the unconscious Principal Tang, who was still in a sitting position on the floor.

"Um, yes," I said, thinking quickly. "Principal Tang wanted to—um—take a nap."

"On the floor?" Mr. Wu said with a skeptical look.

"It's a perfectly good floor to nap on," David snapped, so defensively that the adults looked taken aback by his tone.

"What's with all the mess everywhere?" cried Mrs. Lin, pointing at the school supplies and mashed-up cakes on the ground.

David and I exchanged a quick look. Maybe it was because we'd spent years at each other's throats, studying the other's moves. Whatever the case, I knew exactly what he was thinking. The situation looked very bad for us, and no amount of sweet-talking would get us out of this mess. The only thing left to do was to make a run for it.

"Gotta go!" David shouted. He grabbed my hand.

Together, we fled past the teachers and students, ignoring their cries behind us.

CHAPTER THIRTEEN

The rest of Sunday came and went, mercifully uneventful. Though I waited with a tense, horrified sort of anticipation, there was no indignant call from the Chinese school about the unexplainable mess David and I had left in Principal Tang's office. Hopefully, that meant that after we'd left, the teachers and students had assumed that Principal Tang had created that mess herself before falling asleep near her desk.

Lao Lao reassured me that the principal wouldn't remember what had happened, and that the only aftereffect she'd feel from the class two spirit's possession would be a light headache. Which was good. Really good. If Principal Tang knew what had happened to her, David and I would be in big, big trouble. I wasn't sure what the exact punishment for "using shamanic powers to mess up the principal's office" was, but I didn't want to find out.

There was still the matter of the mason jar containing the wisp of the class two spirit.

"This one, you'll have to return to the spirit realm

yourself," Lao Lao said to me on Monday morning as I was rushing around, getting ready for school. Because of the training we'd been doing together, my grandmother had grown strong enough that she no longer needed to be anchored to Jade as often. This was both a positive development, because it meant we were both growing stronger, and a negative one, because it meant my grandmother was free to trail me around everywhere—and did so. "We need to go to the Department of Supernatural Record-Keeping to send it back. I intend to ask them about what's going on with these spirit attacks, too."

The Department of Supernatural Record-Keeping. Lao Lao spoke about that casually, as though it were the supermarket. "It'll have to wait until after class," I said. "Okay?"

I could tell my grandmother wasn't satisfied with the answer, but she just pursed her lips and nodded. I couldn't cut class to go chase down some place called the Department of Supernatural Record-Keeping. My parents would disown me if they found out.

By Monday afternoon, I could breathe easy again. Aside from the abnormally bad weather, Groton seemed to be back to usual. Once I took this class two spirit back to where it came from, things *would* be normal again.

Then David cornered me in the hall after our English class, the last period of the day. "What are you up to after school?"

"Um . . . studying. And then practicing piano," I said, for the sake of everyone around us who might have been listening in. Then, lowering my voice, I whispered, "I'm going to a place called—um—the Department of Supernatural Record-Keeping to bring the class two spirit back to the spirit realm."

David's eyes lit up behind his lenses as though I'd told him Christmas was coming two months early. "Really? Can I come?"

"I'm not sure," I said honestly. This place sounded top secret, and Lao Lao hadn't said I could invite anyone else there. Technically, David and I were partners now, or at least two undercover shamans who didn't hate each other, but I was so used to us being rude to each other that this politeness business was throwing me for a loop.

"It'll be fun. We can study together after at my place," said David.

Privately, I thought I would rather study in the middle of an erupting volcano. "It's okay. I'll just go ho—"

"And I want to talk to you about, well, the *thingamajig* yesterday," David murmured, lowering his voice. "I think we really need to discuss it."

"Thingamajig?"

David's face twitched. "The spirit attacks. Joe has a theory about why these class one and class two spirits are targeting us specifically." He hissed the last words but didn't speak quietly enough, because we still attracted a weird look from

Matthew Bartleby, who was passing by. Hopefully, Matthew just thought we were talking about a video game.

"Say it louder next time, won't you?" I groaned. "Look, can we . . . can we just reschedule the . . . the *thingamajig* for another time?" My planner was packed, and there was no room for scheduling in a shaman battle.

"Sure thing, and why don't we just reschedule the end of the world while we're at it?"

"Yeah, that'd be great," I said. "Maybe for sometime next month instead. Thanks, David."

"I was being SARCASTIC!" he hollered in my ear.

Backing away, I threw him a disgruntled look and rubbed my poor ear. "Well, you don't have to shout about it."

"Meet me at the Clubhouse of Champions after school," David said stubbornly.

I gave him a blank stare. "The what?"

He blushed. "Oh, right, you wouldn't know. Um . . . that's just what I call my tree house."

The Clubhouse of Champions. I had to hand it to David—there was truly nobody else like him on this planet. In this universe, even.

"Anyway, my place after school, okay? Then we'll head over to the Department together." He hurried off without waiting for me to confirm, as though it were already a done deal.

Piano and homework would have to wait. For a long time, probably.

After the bus dropped me off, I hurried into my house. I headed straight upstairs to my room to grab Jade. Lao Lao was hovering above the rabbit, fast asleep and snoring.

"WAKE UP!" I shouted.

Jade's ears twitched at the sound of my voice. Lao Lao snored once more and then smacked her lips together. She opened her eyes. "Oh, Winnie. Had a good day at school?"

"It was okay, I guess." I scooped up Jade and pressed her warm body close to my chest, and then I grabbed the mason jar with the class two spirit and shoved it into my backpack.

My grandmother seemed wide awake now, as though the idea of going to the Department of Supernatural Record-Keeping had rejuvenated her. She floated behind me as I entered the hall, checking that the coast was clear. Lisa was in her room talking to someone—probably Matt—at the top of her lungs.

I stashed my grandmother's cookbook in my backpack at the last moment, figuring it might come in handy.

"We're going over to David's before heading to the Department of Supernatural Record-Keeping," I informed Lao Lao. "He wants to battle us, I think. Or just tag along and observe. Can't ever tell with that guy."

A thoughtful look entered my grandmother's eye. "Ah, your friend David. Yes, we should take him along. I just hope that old fart Joe has developed manners in the meantime."

It seemed my grandmother actually wanted to hang out

with David. That made one of us. "David's not my friend," I corrected as I bounded down the stairs.

"What's this about David?"

I almost tripped over the last step in shock. Mama, who I hadn't realized was home, stepped out of the kitchen. She had one AirPod in her right ear and held the other in her left hand. She wore a red workout tank and black leggings. Evidently, she'd been meditating.

"I'm—I'm going over to the Clubhouse of Champ— I mean, to David's house," I said quickly, "to . . . study and practice piano. Um, is that okay?"

Part of me—like 99 percent—hoped Mama would say no, and I could just stay here and ignore my magical problems. I crossed my fingers behind my back.

Mama's suspicious expression turned into a beam at the mention of David's name. It figured. My family had always been close to the Zuos, since they'd immigrated here from China. If Mama could have had her way, David and I would have hung out all the time. And I mean *all* the time.

Every few months or so, my family or the Zuos would throw an "Asian party," as I liked to call it, and invite a few other Chinese families around the area to come hang out, drink beer, and play cards. These gatherings always turned out awkward for us kids, who were as young as three to as old as eighteen. We would be forced to make small talk for hours on end until the parents got tired of each other and took us home.

Anyway, point is, Mama *adored* David. She gushed over him in a way that she never gushed over me.

"Of course! Say hi to David's parents for me. Wait—do you want me to give you a ride? My class this afternoon got canceled, so I have time."

"No, that's okay." The last thing I wanted was for my mother to drive me over to David's. No doubt she'd spend an hour complimenting him and asking about Mr. and Mrs. Zuo. My mother was the queen of small talk. "I'll just take my bike. Be back by dinner."

"Stay as long as you'd like!"

"Nope, I'll definitely be back soon," I muttered as I grabbed my bike out of the garage. I didn't intend to stay at David's any longer than necessary. The plan was to be home just in time for dinner.

The bike ride to David's place took about five minutes. He lived just three neighborhoods over, in a respectably sized beige house with a white picket fence. I left my bike in David's driveway and rang the doorbell.

When he answered the door, David did a double take as his gaze fell upon Lao Lao. I guess he still wasn't quite used to seeing spirits yet. Neither was I, really. Joe emerged from over David's shoulder, and Lao Lao gave the old man a cold nod.

"Come in," David said. "My parents are out, so you don't have to worry about us being disturbed."

I obeyed, taking off my shoes and holding them in my hand. We walked through David's house toward the back door.

"This is a very clean house," Lao Lao commented as

we walked into David's spacious living room. There was a grandfather clock propped up next to a grand piano, and across from that, a black couch set. The white walls were decorated with baby pictures of David and fairy lights. There was a tank in a corner of the room, where David's iguana, Qianlong, was lounging among the branches inside. "It's much neater than your room, Winnie."

David snickered, and I frowned. He slid open the back door and put on a pair of sneakers that were directly outside the door.

David's backyard was huge, the lawn grass perfectly green and trimmed. There was one enormous oak tree in the middle of the yard, and in it was the wooden tree house. The tree house was pretty plain, but there was a white sign tacked over the front door that read CLUBHOUSE OF CHAMPIONS in big, bold letters. He really hadn't been kidding.

I followed David as he climbed up the ladder into the tree house.

"Make yourself comfortable," he said, gesturing for me to sit down on the wooden floor.

I took in my surroundings. There were lots of dog-eared books and old newspaper clippings stacked neatly in one corner of the tree house, and a box of granola bars beside them. Next to that was what I could only assume to be an array of makeshift weapons, including a water gun, a spatula, a waffle iron, and a pair of gardening shears. A whiteboard hung on one wall, where David had roughly sketched what appeared to be a map of Groton.

"This place is neater than your room, too, Winnie," said my grandmother, causing Joe to double over with laughter.

"My room isn't even that messy," I protested.

David snorted, too, but quickly stopped when I shot him my nastiest glare. "All right, let's get down to business," David said briskly, sitting down cross-legged on the floor in front of a coffee table. I followed suit. David pointed at me. "You're a shaman. I'm a shaman. What's the source of your power?"

I blinked in confusion. "Er—the source?"

"Like, what unleashed your power?"

"Ohhhh." I pulled Lao Lao's cookbook out of my backpack and passed it over to David, who peered at it curiously. "Mooncakes."

David glanced up from the cookbook to me. Now he was the one who looked confused. Clearly, that wasn't the answer he'd expected. "Moon . . . cakes?"

"Yes, mooncakes. M-O-O-N—"

He threw me a sour look. "I know how to spell, thanks. Just . . . huh. Didn't expect that."

"Well, what's the source of your power?" I asked, feeling self-conscious now.

David reached under the coffee table in front of us and pulled out a large, thin black book. "Calligraphy," he said, passing the book over to me.

"I was known as a master of calligraphy when I was alive," bragged Joe, crossing his arms over his chest. "That's why I sealed my magic in a calligraphy book for my descendants, like you, David."

I took it carefully and flipped through the pages. They were filled with Chinese idioms written in gorgeous, artsy calligraphy, the kind of words that belonged on wall scrolls and in picture frames. "So how do you fight off spirits? Do you paint on them?" I snickered as I pictured David holding a giant calligraphy brush and chasing down loose spirits with it.

He scowled. "No. I'm more advanced, which means that while this calligraphy book unlocked my powers, my true power comes from combining with Joe. He's the source of my power." Joe waved and grinned.

I narrowed my eyes. The dig was subtle, but I'd heard it. David was more advanced than me because he could successfully combine with his overspirit, which I hadn't even come close to yet. I couldn't look at Lao Lao, afraid of the disappointment I might see on her face.

"So shamans get the source of their power from—books?" I said. "Any kind of books?"

My grandmother nodded. "Books, you see, are the most effective means of preserving and passing down knowledge, through storytelling or the conveying of information. That makes them the ideal choice for preserving the art of shamanism."

That made sense. The textbooks at school somehow managed to survive years of kids beating them up and spilling food on them. My impression of books was that they could survive anything, including a zombie apocalypse. Defeating some pesky spirits was probably a walk in the park in comparison.

"So there are more books like this, then?" I asked. "And more shamans in the world? How many?"

"Fifty are officially registered with the Shaman Task Force," said Joe. "Though many more who show talent for shamanism aren't ever selected to join the task force. They stay hidden, so you'll likely never meet the majority of them in your lifetime."

"Groton is special because there's a portal from the human world to the Department of Supernatural Record-Keeping, a go-between place for the human and spirit worlds," Lao Lao explained. "Can you guess where it is?"

Though I wouldn't have had a clue five minutes before, the answer clicked into place almost without my having to think about it. Lao Lao had said that shaman magic could be sealed inside books, and that books were the source of knowledge and power. So, logically, it would make sense for the access to be in one place—

"A bookstore, isn't it?" I said. "The Suntreader." It was the largest independent bookstore in the county, with three levels. It wasn't all that hard to imagine that the Suntreader contained otherworldly secrets, too. The place was certainly big enough for it.

Lao Lao nodded, beaming at me with pride. "Exactly."

"So what are we waiting for? We should just head over

to the Suntreader now," said David, standing up with an impatient expression on his face.

"I think you're both ready to take your training to the next level," agreed Joe. "We have to move quickly. The Spirit Council has confirmed that there's a class three spirit in this town."

"So it *is* the one that's been sending class one and class two spirits after us, then?" Lao Lao's forehead scrunched up. "I knew it. To think that there's a class three spirit targeting us . . . and it's too much of a coward to come after us directly."

I gulped. I'd never faced a class three spirit before. But having fought—and barely defeated—class one and class two spirits, I wasn't in a hurry to fight this new threat.

"Well, class three spirits aren't typically known for their bravery and strength of character," Joe scoffed.

Lao Lao nodded at Joe's words. It seemed, for now at least, that the rivalry between the two overspirits had been set aside. "This spirit is growing stronger, though it's still not strong enough to possess a human body—that's when we'll *really* be in danger. Before that happens, we need to capture the spirit."

David glanced at me, excitement and nervousness in his features. I probably had a similar look on my face.

"We can take this class three spirit, then, can't we?" I said. "Since it's not that strong yet?"

"Who do you think you are? You're not very powerful, either," Lao Lao replied. Oof. Leave it to my grandmother to put me in my place. "Just know that class one and class two spirits are nothing compared to class three spirits, and you'll be in real trouble when you come across one of those."

"What exactly *is* a class three spirit?" David asked, beating me to the question. "Why's it so dangerous?"

"It's the spirit of a legendary figure, such as a hero," explained Lao Lao. "You see, once a person passes into the spirit world, they maintain or even gain power if the people in the human world continue to share their story. That's how class three spirits can grow so powerful, even if they only ever existed in storybooks. Their stories are passed down from generation to generation. In order to capture a class three spirit, you must undertake a process called the Naming. You call the spirit's True Name to seal it back into its story. Now, memorize my next words, for you'll have to recite them as part of the Naming," said Lao Lao, giving us a serious look. "Evil spirit, no longer will you roam freely in this world. By the powers vested in me, I call you by your True Name and command you to return to your story. I name you—" She paused. "Then you say their True Name. Repeat those words back to me."

The two of us obeyed, and Lao Lao nodded in satisfaction when we managed to successfully repeat the Naming back to her after a few failed attempts.

"How do we know a spirit's True Name?" asked David, wide-eyed.

"You don't, unless you've unlocked True Sight." Lao

Lao pursed her lips. "I expect you're both still a ways from achieving that. Hopefully, this class three spirit won't grow too strong in the meantime."

David and I exchanged nervous looks. Yeah, I had a feeling that this spirit wasn't going to politely pause on any of its developing powers just so the two of us could catch up.

"What's True Sight?" I asked.

"True Sight is when you and your overspirit are fully aligned, mentally and emotionally. It's the power that proves your capability to the Spirit Council," said Joe. "True Sight is a crucial step to shaman training that signals that you have the basic foundation to become members of the Shaman Task Force. You'll know when you've achieved it. Typically, shamans unlock True Sight anywhere from twelve hours to twelve years after they begin training."

"Twelve *years*?" groaned David, smacking his forehead. "We don't have twelve years!"

"Ah, that was an outlier," Lao Lao interjected. "The younger you are when you start training, the earlier you'll unlock True Sight. You two don't have to worry about a thing."

"Probably," muttered Joe under his breath.

That was vague and unhelpful, but I was beginning to learn not to expect anything different from grown-ups.

"You both need to take this training seriously," Joe chimed in. His eyes lingered on me, and I quickly looked away. "Class three spirits are clever and evasive, and the most powerful among them can disrupt the fabric of this universe. It'll take more than your wits to capture it even in a weakened state."

"Disrupt the fabric of the *universe?*" David hung his head in his hands. "Oh, fantastic."

"Let's get going to the Department of Supernatural Record-Keeping now," Lao Lao said. "The sooner we get that class two spirit back to the spirit realm, the better."

As David and I headed down the tree house ladder to grab our bikes, my heart hammered. Finally, I had a feeling we were getting some real answers to what was going on in Groton.

I'd always loved going to the Suntreader, but this time was different. This was a new kind of anticipation—an expectation of the supernatural. David and I pedaled along mostly in silence, the spirits floating behind us.

As we turned a corner, there it was, nestled between Subway and Supercuts: the Suntreader, the town's indie bookstore and, apparently, an access point to the spirit realm. It was a green building with a cart of books outside on the sidewalk. Lao Lao stopped and hovered in the air, pressing her fingers to her temples in concentration.

I couldn't help but think the bookstore looked so . . . ordinary.

"You'd never guess anything supernatural was going on

around here," David said. Again, we were on the same wavelength. Again, I hated it.

I was thinking that I'd been meaning to pick up the last volumes of Fruits Basket anyway. Unless a spirit wrecked the Suntreader before I could get to that. But there probably weren't any more evil and chaotic spirits around—at least not here, at this very moment. Right?

The closer we got to the Suntreader, the chillier the air around us seemed to get. It was the same kind of chill I'd gotten around the other spirits before. I gulped, suddenly feeling nervous.

When we headed into the store, I was greeted with the familiar, cozy smell of books. The store had been decorated with colorful leaves, pumpkins, and cinnamon-scented candles. From the ceiling, large, glowing yellow-orange bulbs hung down—hence the store's name, the *Sun*treader.

There were a handful of people browsing the bookshelves, about the same number as usual. Mr. Stevens, the bald owner of the bookshop, was putting some books onto the shelves. There was no evil spirit in sight, nor anything that looked remotely supernatural.

"So what do we do now?" David asked, glancing toward the spirits with a clueless expression on his face.

"Ask the owner to take you to the eighty-eighth floor," said Joe.

I stared at him as though he'd told us to fly to Jupiter. He might as well have. "There's no such thing. This store only has three levels."

"The eighty-eighth floor," insisted the old spirit, scowling at me as though miffed I couldn't follow basic directions. "I said what I said, lassie."

I glanced toward David for help, but he just shrugged. Useless.

Lao Lao zipped around the store, but before I could attempt to follow her, Mr. Stevens turned and spotted me. He smiled and raised a hand in greeting. "Ah, Winnie. You've brought a friend today." He nodded at David, his eyes skimming over the spirits—of course, he couldn't see them. "Back for more manga?"

Back to visit your eighty-eighth floor that may or may not exist, actually. Oh, did I mention I have shaman powers now? Anyway, how are the wife and kids? Nope, definitely couldn't say that.

I managed a smile. "Not today, actually. I'm, um, I need to go to the eighty-eighth floor."

The smile froze on Mr. Stevens's face, and embarrassment began to flood me. Great. Joe had led me astray, and now the store owner thought I'd lost my marbles. I was about to make a run for it when Mr. Stevens's expression cleared. He looked as blank as my classmates did on the day of an algebra test. "Ah, yes. Follow me." Mr. Stevens gestured for us to follow him, and made his way toward the elevator in the back of the store.

"Yo, this is wild," David whispered.

We followed Mr. Stevens, passing the fantasy section and then the manga section. One glance around the store had shown nothing out of the ordinary, and that chilly feeling was leaving the longer I lingered in the warmth of the cozy bookstore. A nearby mother and son acknowledged us with a friendly wave, but other than that, nobody in the bookstore seemed to notice our strange little party making our way to the back. Though, of course, they couldn't even see Lao Lao and Joe.

"Eighty-eighth floor, coming up," said Mr. Stevens in that serene voice. He gave us an empty smile and pressed the "up" button. The doors dinged open, and he gestured for us to get in. When we did, Mr. Stevens pressed an elevator button labeled 88, which I'd never noticed before, right above the button for the third floor.

"You're telling me this floor was here all along, and I never noticed it?" I burst out incredulously. It didn't seem possible. Countless hours I'd spent browsing the shelves of the Suntreader, carefully selecting my next book haul—and I'd missed the fact that there was an eighty-eighth floor in this place?

"There's an eight hundred and eighty-eighth floor, too. But that one will only be visible to shamans who unlock True Sight," explained my grandmother.

I was still trying to process the fact that there was an eighty-eighth floor, not to mention an *eight hundred and eighty-eighth floor.*

"It's the ultimate power any shaman can possess. You'll know when you've achieved it," said Joe mysteriously. "Just know that you're both a long, *long* way off from obtaining True Sight. Think as far away as Earth is from Pluto."

That was encouraging to hear.

"It's amazing what things you'll notice when your eyes have been opened to the supernatural," said Lao Lao.

"Human eyesight is so limited," Joe agreed.

"Winnie, I can see your *skeleton*!" shouted David, pointing at me.

I let out a scream that I wasn't entirely proud of. "What?!"

"I'm kidding. You should see the look on your face."

"You—!"

David's obnoxious laughter was cut off when the elevator shot upward at top speed. I might have found it funny if I hadn't been busy screaming again, this time out of true fear. Even the spirits were screaming. It felt like the contents of my stomach had shot up into my throat, and I clung to the railing for dear life.

A few horrible seconds later, the elevator lurched to a stop. "Eighty-eighth floor," came the soothing announcement over the elevator speaker, and the doors opened. "Department of Supernatural Record-Keeping."

CHAPTER FOURTEEN

The eighty-eighth floor appeared similar to the other floors of the bookstore—with one key difference. The books were floating inside the bookshelves, and each glowed as though it contained some mysterious power. There was an impossible number of books in this space, and the shelves stretched on for what I suspected was forever. Uniformed men and women were positioned between each of the shelves, guarding them with a spear in hand. When I looked closer, I realized with a jolt that they weren't real people— at least, not like any I'd seen before. These people were two-dimensional. They might have stepped right out of a book themselves.

At the front, sitting behind the checkout counter, was a woman who had the head and paws of a cat. She glanced up at the sight of us, pushing her glasses higher on the bridge of her nose. She wore librarian-type glasses—you know, the kind with the dangling chain.

"Welcome to the Department of Supernatural Record-Keeping," said the cat lady, in a voice that sounded perfectly human, so much so that the contrast with her catlike appearance was jarring. "You've come at a good time, as we haven't had much traffic today. I hope you find what you're looking for. Please let me know if I can be of service."

You'd think that after all I'd seen and heard recently, I wouldn't even blink twice at the sight of the cat lady, but I *really* hadn't expected to stumble upon something like that.

"Wh-wh-wh-where are we?" I stammered.

"Haven't you been paying attention at all?" grumbled Joe. "You'd better, because shamans are expected to report here when they've captured spirits. This is the Department of Supernatural Record-Keeping. The woman behind the counter is Xiao Mao, head of the Record-Keeping Task Force."

"Grand Master, it's an honor to have you visit today," continued Xiao Mao as she nodded at Lao Lao, and I was stunned to see her bow her head at my grandmother, as though to someone incredibly important.

Lao Lao smiled graciously. I stared between the two of them, feeling like I was missing something big.

"Lao Lao, why did she call you Grand Master?" I whispered.

"Ah, that's my former title from my much younger days," chuckled my grandmother. "When I was a little older than you, I won the Shaman Junior Tournament. You'll hear more about that tournament, I suspect, in the coming months."

"Your grandmother was not just a shaman—she was the *best* shaman in her day," said Xiao Mao.

My head reeled with the knowledge that not only was there a tournament for shamans but that my grandmother was a former champion. I gazed at Lao Lao with renewed respect. Joe was rolling his eyes a lot, and David's jaw had dropped.

"Big deal," Joe huffed. "I would've won my tournament, too—"

"Except you overslept and missed the preliminary rounds," Xiao Mao said. "And then you tried to enter late, while still wearing your jammies. That was funny. They didn't stop talking about that for years."

Joe's scowl deepened, and Lao Lao cracked up so hard that she doubled over. Even David couldn't resist a grin.

"Anyway, that's neither here nor there," said Lao Lao after she'd recovered from her fit of laughter, though she was still grinning widely. "We can reminisce about the old days later. Right now there's an urgent matter to handle. . . . David, where are you going?" My grandmother's voice turned sharp.

David had dashed over to the nearest row of books. One of the books opened of its own accord, revealing sharp teeth that snapped at his fingers. David shrieked and stumbled into one of the guards, who grunted and pushed him away.

"Ah, yes, some of the books will bite. Don't touch them, please," Xiao Mao said, her voice still serene. "Those books are friendly, but they will bite if they feel threatened."

I got the feeling nothing rattled her. Probably nothing would rattle me, either, if I were a woman with a cat's head.

As if to illustrate her point, one of the guards positioned himself in front of the books protectively, glaring at David.

"What's the big deal?" David asked, annoyed.

"At the Department of Supernatural Record-Keeping, we ask that you please do not touch any book except the one you're looking for," said Xiao Mao. "The Paper Guard will escort any rule-breaking patrons to the exit."

David turned around with a scowl but didn't put up any more fuss.

"The Paper Guard?" I said as the man shifted back into his position.

"They protect these books with their lives," explained Xiao Mao. She turned her eyes toward me, the vertical black pupils seeming to pierce straight through my soul. I suddenly felt nervous, even though I hadn't done anything wrong. "It's a very dangerous but prestigious job."

"How can a bookstore get dangerous?" I was pretty sure the bookstore was the most peaceful place on Earth.

"There are many villainous beings that would steal knowledge for their dastardly means," Joe answered. "For example, when I ruled over China—"

"We're here to return this class two spirit back to the spirit realm," explained Lao Lao, cutting off his explanation. Joe threw my grandmother an irritated look, but then just huffed and turned away. "Put the jar on the counter, Winnie."

I held up the jar and placed it on the counter. Xiao Mao

picked it up with a paw and turned it over, lowering her glasses and squinting at the spirit. Then she began muttering to herself. "Ah, I see. Class two spirit, newly crossed, has a peanut allergy . . ."

"Remember how we discussed that books are special because they preserve knowledge?" asked Lao Lao as Xiao Mao continued examining the spirit trapped inside the jar. David and I nodded. "The Department of Supernatural Record-Keeping oversees *all* the special books that contain precious stories that have been passed down for generations. These stories depict legendary figures that live in the spirit realm. If given the opportunity, these spirits can pass through the pages of the storybook and into the human world. That's where shamans step in, to make sure that when that does happen, the spirits are sent back to the spirit realm, where they belong."

As my grandmother spoke, the cat lady nodded along. "There are many branches of the Department within libraries and bookstores across the nation," Xiao Mao said. "This is the newest one. Hence, why we need two new shamans on board to guard this branch. I *did* ask for more experienced ones from the Shaman Task Force, but alas . . . the Spirit Council seemed to have faith that two new shamans-in-training would be up to the task." She shrugged, but her demeanor made it clear that she would've preferred shamans who had more experience under their belt.

"The Shaman Task Force has been short-staffed lately,"

said Lao Lao. "But rest assured that these two are more than capable of learning the ropes fast." She gave David and me a rare grin.

Xiao Mao didn't look convinced, which didn't exactly boost my confidence. She finally set down the jar and typed something into the computer in front of her, her long claws clacking against the keys. After she squinted at the screen, she abruptly got up and headed toward the back of the bookstore. She reappeared a few moments later with a large, worn black book. Luckily, this one didn't have teeth, but there was a giant hole in the middle of it. I watched curiously as Xiao Mao opened the jar and dumped the essence of the class two spirit into the hole. There was a faint wailing noise, as though the spirit was complaining, and then the hole sealed shut, repairing the book.

"There," said Xiao Mao crisply. She flashed a smile, baring her canines. "That spirit's back where it belongs now." She snapped her fingers, and a nearby guard rolled a cart toward her. She placed the book onto the cart and whispered something to the guard, and the guard rolled the cart back down the aisle.

"Thank you, Xiao Mao," Lao Lao said.

"Of course. These two kittens—I mean, children—they're doing a good job so far." She nodded at us, but her eyes remained cold and calculating. "Though we'll be watching from here and judging whether they'll make worthy additions to the Shaman Task Force."

"Don't worry," said Joe. "What these kids lack in skill, they make up for in enthusiasm."

I frowned. David's expression turned sour, too. Okay, so maybe we weren't exactly up to par yet, but we'd only been doing this shaman thing for a few days. I could see where my parents' ridiculously high expectations came from. Lao Lao had clearly set the standard. Besides—all these adults were making my decisions for me, when I hadn't even decided yet if I wanted to be part of the Shaman Task Force.

"Ah—one more question," said Lao Lao. "You wouldn't happen to know any details about a class three spirit roaming around in Groton, would you? A spirit that sent this class two spirit after us?"

The cat lady blinked slowly. "My job is only to keep track of these books," she said. "My orders from the Spirit Council are to not interfere with shamans and their training. But I will say that with the Mid-Autumn Festival approaching, there has been plenty of . . . *activity* of late."

David and I exchanged a look. It sounded like the Spirit Council was testing us. And even if Xiao Mao's response had been cryptic, she'd hinted that there was something going on, something related to the upcoming holiday. The Mid-Autumn Festival was just around the corner—in one week, to be exact. That hardly gave us any time to prepare for supernatural happenings. I gulped, feeling nervous. Hopefully, I was just being paranoid. Lao Lao and Joe were already heading toward the elevator, indicating that it was time to go.

"Thank you," called my grandmother.

I mumbled a thank-you as well and glanced back at Xiao Mao as I left. But she was transfixed by her computer screen, her claws typing madly away.

CHAPTER FIFTEEN

"So, what did you want to talk about?" I asked David. It was the next day, and we were both seated at David's dining room table, surrounded by our homework. I was looking up more about the legend behind the Mid-Autumn Festival, potentially as a topic for the mythology presentation. I also wanted to see if I could find any information that might help David and me if evil spirits did stir during the holiday.

Joe was taking a nap in the living room. Lao Lao swept about the kitchen, examining every nook and cranny, stopping here and there to exclaim over the Zuos' state-of-the-art kitchen equipment.

"Ah, Hou Yi," said my grandmother. Her voice drifted from somewhere above my shoulder, startling me. I hadn't realized she'd drawn so close. "What a great story that is. Though, unfortunately, the actual figure of Hou Yi is more mischievous than the stories would have you believe, and..." Lao Lao's voice trailed off, and her eyebrows scrunched together as if she'd been struck by a sudden thought.

"Lao Lao?"

My grandmother shook her head, as though freeing herself from the thought, and then drifted off from us again.

"We can talk about the mythology presentation later," said David. He fixed me with a serious stare that made him look about twenty years older. "So I've had some time to think about this . . . this Shaman Task Force stuff since yesterday. And I . . . I realized that whatever is happening to us, to this town, is probably huge. It's bigger than any petty little feuds we might've had in the past."

"Define 'petty.'"

"I want us to train together, Winnie. Like, seriously train."

"Isn't that what we're doing right now?" I pointed down at our homework.

"I mean train together to defeat this loose class three spirit—if there is one—and prove ourselves to the Spirit Council. If we join the Shaman Task Force and team up whenever spirits are on the loose, we'll be unstoppable. We'll be the heroes of Groton." David gave a solemn nod, as though preparing himself to commit to some noble cause. "We should probably talk costume design while we're at it. Superheroes always have the neatest costumes."

Ooooooookay. I realized David must've cracked under the stress of our looming tests and piano recital. "David, hold up. I still don't know if I'm going to join the Shaman Task Force."

"What?" he exclaimed, as if I'd announced I was moving to the North Pole.

"I'm just not sure I can do this shaman thing, long-term. It sounds like a big commitment. It might be better if you handle it."

Lao Lao coughed behind me. "Now, look, Winnie—"

But David interrupted her. An incredulous expression rose to his face, like he couldn't believe his ears. "What do you mean, you aren't going to do this shaman thing?" he burst out. "Who else *can* do this besides us?"

"I mean I'm looking at this as, like, a contract job."

"Being a member of the Shaman Task Force isn't like one of those free trial offers," Lao Lao sniffed, looking offended. "You can't try it out and then cancel when you decide you don't want it."

"I know that," I mumbled, even though I'd been thinking about this shaman gig exactly like one of those free trial offers.

"You've already proven that you *do* have what it takes to step up to the task, capturing a class one *and a* class two spirit. I don't understand the problem."

I bit my lip, swallowing back some of the conflicting emotions that were warring inside me. Yeah, I knew I should do the right thing, the *heroic* thing, and announce that I was going to dedicate my life to the Shaman Task Force and fight evil until my dying breath. And truthfully, there was a part of me that wanted to train my shaman powers and prove myself as capable and brilliant as my grandmother.

But, well, if there was a class three spirit on the loose and targeting us, it would have been causing a lot more chaos in Groton. Right? After we'd sent the class two spirit back to the Department of Supernatural Record-Keeping, there had been nothing vile stirring in Groton, aside from the cafeteria meat loaf.

If I was being honest with myself, though, the real reason I couldn't throw myself into training was that I was *scared*. Scared that I wouldn't be as good at being a shaman as I was at playing the piano, and that David would prove himself to be better than me yet again. He was already better than me at Chinese, piano, and pretty much everything else. I couldn't stand the thought of being compared to him in shaman duties, too. I was scared that I would bear the weight of a huge responsibility, only to let down the entire *world*. I couldn't even let go of the fear of letting down my family.

I just wanted Mama and Baba to be proud of me for once, instead of David.

"I don't know if I'm that interested in fighting evil spirits," I lied. "It's stressful, all right? And it's not like anybody in the human world is paying me or even knows it's me doing the fighting." At least if they knew my identity, I could look forward to fan mail, a TV show, lots of TikTok followers, that sort of thing.

"But—but—" David spluttered, his mouth moving and making a choked sound. "But you—*we* have to do this saving-the-world thing! We have special powers, and we have to use them for good. That's what superheroes are supposed to do."

"Yeah, well, I'm not like those superheroes," I retorted. Those superheroes didn't have strict parents who thought getting straight A's was more important than saving the world. Didn't have to go to Chinese school on the weekends, or be the best at piano, or any of that. "I've got my hands full just trying to do everything my parents already expect of me, without having to save the world from evil spirits. You of all people should understand."

David sat back and slid down in his seat, looking thunderstruck. He fell silent, but there was accusation in his expression. I knew he was upset that I was turning my back on this.

Lao Lao seized the opening to interject. "Winnie, think this through," my grandmother said sternly. "Wouldn't it be worse for your grades if your school was destroyed?"

I let out a long sigh. "I don't know if I want to dedicate myself to hunting down evil spirits. The only thing I want to hunt down is a college scholarship."

"It's a little more complicated than that," my grandmother said in a gentle but firm voice.

"Yeah," agreed David. "I think you have better odds of hunting down a spirit than a college scholarship."

I stared at David and then Lao Lao, and then back at David. The silence stretched on, and David's grin slowly fell.

I wished I could have been as willing as David clearly

was to sign up for the Shaman Task Force. But . . . I don't know. Maybe I'd have done it if I'd thought I could juggle that on top of everything else. But the more I thought about it, the more I didn't really see that happening. It's not like my superpower was the ability to do a million things at once. I guess the ability to balance shaman duties on top of other responsibilities was another area where David bested me.

"Sorry, I don't think so." I was careful not to look at either of them so I wouldn't see the disappointment on their faces. "You might be able to handle being town superhero on top of all your other responsibilities, but I'm not sure I can."

"Winnie—"

"I've just got too much going on, all right? Lao Lao, you can have David fulfill my shaman duties instead," I said, still staring at my feet. David would probably do a better job than me anyway. "See? It all works out perfectly. David can for sure take down a class three spirit on his own."

"But—"

I cut David off. Though my heart was sinking, I knew this was for the best. "You win. Okay? I'll see you around."

Ignoring David's protests, I gathered up my possessions. I strode down the hall toward the door—and almost crashed right into someone who was coming through the doorway.

"Whoa! Who're you?" shouted Luke, David's older brother. He was in Lisa's year in high school, and the complete opposite of his nerd brother. From what Lisa said, Luke had played on the basketball team all through middle school and was one of the most popular guys in the grade.

Luke blinked and squinted down at me. He was *really* tall, like two heads taller than me. I had to crane my neck, and I felt like I was staring up at a giant. "Um, hi."

Luke's eyes brightened with recognition. "Oh, hey. Winnie, right? You're the Zengs' kid."

I nodded. "I'm just leaving."

Luke ran a hand through his hair as he stepped aside. "Um—and your sister. Lisa," he blurted out, his cheeks reddening. "How is she?"

Luke had always had a thing for Lisa for as far back as I could remember. I didn't see why. Luke was tall and cool, and Lisa was . . . Lisa. Some mysteries of the universe just weren't meant to be solved.

"Oh, you know, she's . . . Lisa." And without wasting another moment, I rushed out the door, but not before I heard Luke's voice behind me as he spoke to David.

"You chasing girls out of the house now, little bro? They grow up so fast. . . ."

As I grabbed my bike to head back to my house, Lao Lao immediately started scolding me. I put my helmet on, trying hard not to pay my grandmother any mind, but it was like trying to drown out the noise of the ocean. A really loud ocean that was currently yelling in my ear.

"When I was your age, I served the Spirit Council

dutifully as a member of the Shaman Task Force. I protected my city from all sorts of evil spirits. You need to be more mature, Winnie. You—"

"Well, I'm sorry I'm not more *mature*, okay?" I burst out, whirling around to glare at Lao Lao. My grandmother fell silent, maybe as surprised by my outburst as I was. "I'm sorry. Maybe things would be better if *David* were your grandkid."

"That's not true," Lao Lao said, looking stunned. "Why would you say that?"

I knew it wasn't true, and yet I couldn't help the sharp words that poured out of my mouth. Even if Lao Lao didn't wish David were her grandchild instead of me, I was pretty sure my parents wouldn't be opposed if brilliant David and I were swapped one day. That was why they always compared me to him. Right?

"I'm not you, Lao Lao. And we're not living in Shanghai. Things are different here in Michigan, okay? I have a lot of other responsibilities on my plate, like school and piano. And I don't need anything else that makes me *weird* around here." I already stood out for being one of the few Asian kids in my class. And for eating "strange" food sometimes. Add shaman magic on top of that, and I could be a whole circus act on my own. The Winnie Zeng Freak Show.

"There is no bigger responsibility than protecting your city," my grandmother insisted, lips pursed. "The Spirit

Council once selected me for this most important role, and now they've seen the potential in you as my youngest grandchild. It is an *honor*."

"Yeah, well, you can tell the Spirit Council to give that honor to someone else. Maybe Lisa. I don't want it." It was a lie, and I wasn't totally sure why I said it. But the thought that I couldn't live up to everyone's expectations—couldn't live up to Lao Lao's expectations? Maybe, in this case, it was better not to try.

There was a long, tense silence that stretched out between Lao Lao and me. Finally, she asked, "That's your final answer? You won't change your mind?"

"No, I won't," I said savagely, though at the disappointed expression on my grandmother's face, the smallest bit of regret twisted in the pit of my stomach. Just a teeny, tiny ounce of it.

"Fine," Lao Lao said. She didn't sound angry at me. Actually, she just shook her head as though disheartened, and somehow that made me feel a million times worse. "There's no point in lingering around here, then. I can't convince you to do something you don't want to do. I'll go back to the spirit realm."

"Wait. You have to go back?"

"What's the point of staying here without a shaman to train?" There was scorn in my grandmother's voice, and beneath that, I thought I heard disappointment. "Well, that's not the only reason. I ... I have a sudden hunch about what's been going on in Groton. If I'm correct, then we'll know how to capture this rogue spirit, even though you haven't unlocked True Sight yet. I need to check my theory by returning to the spirit world." A thoughtful expression rose to Lao Lao's face.

Something caught in my throat. I didn't want my grandmother to leave so suddenly, though I knew I had no business feeling regretful, since I was the one who'd decided against shaman training. Of course Lao Lao couldn't stay here without a reason. "Are you . . . going to come back?"

"Once I've confirmed my theory—or not," my grandmother sighed. "But I can't promise I'll be lingering around here often, unless I find a new shaman to train."

And to replace you. The words were silent, but I heard them loudly all the same.

"Goodbye, Winnie."

Before I could manage another word, the spirit of my grandmother shot up into the sky. David's front door opened and he came running out of the house, but it was too late to do anything.

"Nice work, Winnie," David grumbled, but he went quiet when I shot him a glare.

We watched in silence as Lao Lao's spirit vanished into thin air. I didn't know what theory Lao Lao had gone off to confirm, but I hoped she'd return soon, even if she was still mad at me. I already missed her presence.

Fall in Groton meant raking fallen leaves into piles just to jump into them and mess them all up again, causing the cranky old man who lived next door to shake his fist at you. It meant driving an hour north to pick a fresh, juicy batch of apples at one of the best apple orchards in the state. It meant bumpy hayrides, yummy cinnamon doughnuts, and long lines of suburban soccer moms with their teenage daughters lining up for pumpkin spice lattes at the local Starbucks.

Unfortunately, this year fall had been cold—much colder than usual, forcing students to dig out their winter coats earlier than they were used to. The school halls were filled with the sounds of sneezes and bless-yous, which soon turned into students missing classes because they'd developed colds or fevers. This happened every year at school, but this year it seemed to have happened much quicker, affecting more students and staff. My PE teacher and English teacher *and* science teacher were all out at the same time. It was so bad that the principal had to make an announcement over the loudspeaker asking students and staff to be extra careful with practicing hygiene and not to come to school if they felt even a teeny bit sick.

Fall also meant I had to worry about my piano recital and my English presentation. And if that wasn't enough for one sixth grader to deal with, the Groton Middle School teachers seemed to have conspired to make our lives miserable and had piled on the work this week. On Monday, the pre-algebra teacher, Mr. Yeller, had assigned us a fifty-problem assignment. My Spanish teacher, Mrs. Espinosa, wanted a five-page short story written entirely in Spanish, due by Friday.

"Why are all our teachers so crabby?" I heard Jessamyn asking Tracy in the hallway before fifth period. She sniffled. Her words were coming out all congested, like her nose was stuffed up. "I swear dey're going out of dere way to be ebil and—*ouch!*"

"What?" Tracy said, sounding alarmed.

"You poked be wit your dotebook!"

"It wasn't on purpose—"

"Well, it still *hurt!*"

"What's up with you?" grumbled Tracy. "If you're asking me, the one who's acting crabby around here is *you,* Jessamyn."

If Jessamyn had a retort, it was lost in the loud sneeze she let out.

If the popular girls arguing among themselves wasn't a sign that things were going south around here, then I didn't know *what* was.

The mood at Groton Middle School had turned as gloomy as the weather. I knew middle school would be harder than elementary school, but this was, like, next-level torture. What was going *on?*

I'd never been "stressed out" before, but Lisa complained about it all the time, and I was pretty sure that I now had a good idea of what that felt like.

Speaking of Lisa, my sister was so busy running around from school to softball practice to SAT tutoring that I barely glimpsed her these days, and when I did, she looked worse for the wear. She'd even given up on her blue eye shadow.

On Wednesday evening, when we were sitting at the dining table doing our homework together, I asked Lisa to pass the pencil sharpener. She practically snapped at me.

"How am I supposed to ace my SATs with my kid sister interrupting me all the time?" Lisa snarled. Her eyes were all red and watery, which could have been a side effect of stress or a cold.

"I asked you *one* question," I protested. "And I'm not some little kid. I'm eleven years old!"

Giving me a sneer that could've reduced even the meanest spirit to tears, Lisa grabbed the box of tissues beside her, gathered her belongings, and stormed off from the table without another word.

There it was again—that cold, cold chill that swept through the room, even though the window was shut tight. It caused me to shiver, and I thought it might even have rattled my bones. I wrapped my sweater more tightly around me. No way did I want to be the next one to catch the cold or whatever it was that was going around Groton.

"What is up with everyone lately?" I mumbled. I sighed

and glanced down at my pre-algebra paper. I'd only gotten through five problems so far, and I was pretty sure four of them were wrong. I definitely would regret this the next day, but I decided to give up for the night and finish the evening by practicing piano. Or maybe by sobbing into a pillow. Either seemed likely at this point.

When I stepped into the living room, my eyes were drawn immediately to Jade, who was huddled in the corner of her rabbit pen. She'd barely touched the carrots and lettuce leaves I'd left out for her in the afternoon. Her white coat was shivering. It was as though she, too, felt the unnatural chill in the air.

"Hey, Jade?" I knelt and pushed the bowl of food toward her, but she just scooted back farther into the corner. "What's wrong?" A pang struck my chest when I realized what it might be. "Do you miss Lao Lao?"

I tried not to think about my grandmother, but I couldn't help it. The thought of her—and our last fight—kept creeping into my mind. Since my grandmother had stormed off back to the spirit world, I hadn't heard a word from her. It seemed she hadn't yet been able to confirm or disprove her theory. I could have gone to the Department of Supernatural Record-Keeping to look for her—and the thought had crossed my mind several times—but I was too ashamed, not to mention preoccupied with schoolwork. It was all my fault that my grandmother had left and that she no longer wanted to speak to me. What if, while in the spirit realm, she'd decided she wasn't coming back, ever?

"I miss Lao Lao, too," I admitted, swiping a tear that trickled down my cheek.

"Oh my god. Are you talking to the *rabbit*?"

I turned around so fast I almost gave myself whiplash. Lisa, who was halfway up the stairs with an orange in her hand, snickered at me. I hadn't heard her come back down to grab a snack.

"You're such a freak, Winnie."

That did it. The chill gripped me, and it squeezed my heart. My vision turned red with anger. My sister knew how stressed I was, but she still wouldn't leave me alone. She was older than me, but she never acted mature.

If that's how Lisa wanted to play it, then I wouldn't hold back, either.

"Well, at least I'm not the one who's *dating* a freak!" I spat.

Lisa's face contorted with anger, and some horrible part of me purred in satisfaction at the sight. She opened her mouth to retort but was interrupted.

"*Who's* dating?"

Uh-oh. Mama stomped into the room. She'd already showered and changed into her pink bathrobe and bunny slippers for the night, but that didn't make her any less intimidating, with her arms crossed over her chest and an angry expression on her face.

Pro tip: never infuriate an Asian mother. It might be the last thing you ever do.

Lisa, stricken with fear, almost missed a step and tumbled

down the stairs. She reached out and gripped the banister, hard.

But I wasn't done yet. "It's Lisa," I accused coldly, barely recognizing my own voice as I spoke.

A vindictive pleasure rose from inside me. After all, was it *really* wrong to tell my parents the truth, even if it meant breaching my sister's trust? She shouldn't have been lying and sneaking around in the first place. And asking me to hide this from our parents was wrong of her. Besides, there was a tiny part of me that gloated in this—that knew that if I revealed the truth to Mama and Baba, they'd be furious with Lisa, and glad that I'd told them what was really going on. When they compared us, they'd see *me* as the better daughter.

That part of me wanted my parents to approve of me as the perfect daughter, even now, above all else.

"Lisa's been dating a boy named Matt Zingerman in secret," I said. "Ask her."

A mixture of horror and hurt at being betrayed rose to Lisa's face. The instant I finished speaking, guilt shot through me. But it was too late to take back my words now. The damage was done.

Mama's eyes widened in shock. Her lips parted, then shut. She rounded on my sister, putting her hands on her hips. "Is this true, Lisa? You're dating somebody?"

"I . . . I . . . n-no."

"Then why did Winnie say that you are? Tell the truth,

Lisa. I want the truth. *Now.*" My mother's voice shook with fury. It even made me shrink back. Now I'd fully realized what I'd done.

I didn't think it was right for Lisa to sneak around behind our parents' backs, but that didn't make it right for me to tell on her this way, either. My stomach went queasy. I felt sick inside.

To my shock, Lisa began crying. I couldn't remember the last time I'd seen her shed tears; I thought her tear ducts had disappeared during puberty. She normally seemed so strong and unbreakable to me. Now, though, my older sister's outer surface had shattered.

"I hate you, Winnie!" Lisa shouted, and then ran up the stairs. Mama followed her, scolding her all the way.

Lisa's scream finally shook me out of my strange, icy state. I clapped a hand over my mouth, horror-struck at what I'd done. I was filled with regret. My stomach gave a sickening drop. I shouldn't have done that. I *really* shouldn't have done that.

No matter how angry Lisa had made me, no matter if it was wrong that she was sneaking around behind my parents' back, no matter how stressed out I was right now, I never should've blurted out my sister's secret like that. Lisa had trusted me to keep her secret for her. I'd betrayed her trust—all for a moment of getting my parents' approval against her. And it hadn't been worth it in the least.

What the heck was *wrong* with me?

The sounds of Mama and Lisa arguing upstairs grew louder. To drown everything out, I focused on practicing my recital piece, Rachmaninov's Elégie. For once, playing the piano was the least awful part of my day.

That's how I knew things were getting really bad around here.

CHAPTER SIXTEEN

Lisa went from tossing snarky comments at me to ignoring me entirely. At first I viewed this development as an improvement, since the snubbing was still a step up from the sniping. But I had to admit that the novelty of being invisible wore off quickly.

The worst part was knowing I deserved to be frozen out. I hadn't been nice about revealing the truth to Mama. At all. I wouldn't have been surprised if Lisa never spoke to me ever again.

Between Lisa acting like I didn't exist, and me having a tough time making any friends at Groton Middle School, life really wasn't looking so great. The Mid-Autumn Festival was just a handful of days away, but I'd never been in less of a mood to celebrate anything.

I began sitting by myself at lunch. I couldn't even summon the energy to talk back to David. That was the sign that I'd hit rock bottom.

Even *David* had a cooler crowd to sit with—although that crowd was only slightly cooler and consisted of the kids from math club. Oh yeah, I should mention that David and

I weren't talking anymore, either. That was an improvement in my quality of life, I tried to remind myself. In fact, I would've been happy if he kept up the silent treatment forever. *Totally* happy.

By the time the piano recital rolled around on Saturday, I was ready—more ready than I'd ever been for anything else in my life. Since nobody was talking to me, I'd had no distractions, and I'd been able to concentrate fully on throwing myself into practicing my piece. I was ready to wipe the floor with David and everyone else performing at the recital. Even though it wasn't technically a competition.

I woke up early and put on a simple black dress that my mother had snagged from—you guessed it—T.J. Maxx. On sale, no less. I'm telling you, when it came to bargains, nobody navigated them better than Mama.

Then I put on one-inch heels. Just that one-inch boost would make me slightly taller than David. It would allow me to look down my nose at him as I swept past him after delivering the performance of a lifetime. These encouraging thoughts kept me going through life's many trials.

I bounded down the stairs into the kitchen, where Mama was making breakfast. The air smelled like fried carbs. I could guess from the scent what she was making. "Yóu tiáo!" I shouted in delight at the sight of the dough twists sizzling in the frying pan. Sort of like doughnuts but savory, they had crispy skin and were absolutely scrumptious.

"Your favorite," Mama said with a smile. "Eat up. This will give you lots of energy for your big day."

"You should've told me you were planning to make them," I said. "I would've helped."

"I had Lisa help me earlier instead."

"Lisa?"

As though she'd been summoned by our talking about her, Lisa waltzed into the kitchen. Her scowl deepened when her gaze landed on me. "If I knew the yóu tiáo was for *her*," she said icily, pointing at me, "I wouldn't have gotten up so early to make them."

"Don't be silly. The yóu tiáo is for everyone to share," said my mother. "Also, don't be rude to your sister."

"Sister? What sister? All I see is a snitch," Lisa muttered, loud enough for us to hear. Then she let out a wet cough. My sister was looking worse for the wear these days, just like half the people in this town.

I winced. Lisa's words stung, because I couldn't even deny them. And nobody likes a sibling who's a tattletale.

"Lisa! Don't call your sister a snitch. Go wait in the car if you're going to act like this."

Mama rarely got angry, and it was even more rare for her to raise her voice. But when she got upset, dang, she got *really* upset. Her chest heaved up and down, and her eyes flashed. She gripped the wooden spatula in her hand like she wanted nothing better than to smack Lisa with it. She probably would have, if Lisa hadn't turned on her heel and stormed out of the house.

That gloomy feeling was back. I could feel it hanging thick in the air, like an ugly, invisible force that was squeezing us all from the inside, making us think and say and do hurtful things.

I'd woken up nervous and excited for the piano recital, eager to finally show off what I'd been working on for months. Now all I wanted was for my family and everyone else to stop fighting. I couldn't wait for the day to be over.

The ten-minute car ride over to the high school auditorium was unpleasant. Lisa was still giving me the silent treatment. She only broke it to yell at me to roll my window up, and then once again to mention for the gazillionth time that she'd rather be doing anything else than going to my piano recital.

"I don't see why *I* have to be at Winnie's piano thing," Lisa grumbled, unwrapping a cough drop and popping it into her mouth. "You guys do know I have my practice SAT exam tomorrow, right? I should be focusing on that."

"You'll have plenty of time to study in the afternoon and evening," Baba pointed out.

"This piano recital is extremely important to Winnie," my mother chimed in. "We're all going to cheer her on. *All* of us."

"Winnie, Winnie, Winnie." The way Lisa whined my name made it sound so ugly. "Everything is about Winnie."

Everything was so *not* about me. Maybe if Lisa were nicer to us and actually acted like a good older sister, she'd see that her family *wanted* to be there for her. But she never let us. Instead, she turned everything into an argument or a competition. Instead of ever hanging out with me, Lisa only hung out with Matt, who, no offense, wasn't even good company.

Through gritted teeth, I said, "It's not like I even wanted you to come in the first place."

"That's enough, Winnie!" Mama shouted, turning around in her seat to glare at me, and then fixed Lisa with her glare as well for good measure. "Dear, you say something, too." She whirled accusingly to Baba.

"Stop fighting, girls," Baba said with a sigh, his voice lacking any conviction. He'd come home really late the night before. I only knew this because I'd woken up in the middle of the night to use the toilet and heard him fixing himself a meal in the kitchen.

"They fight like this because you're never around to discipline them," Mama snapped.

I resisted the urge to chime in and point out that the real reason Lisa and I couldn't get along was because they compared us all the time. That would go over *super* well.

"Oh, so now it's my fault that I'm putting meals on the table?" Baba retorted.

"*I'm* putting meals on the table, too!"

"Great. Now our parents are fighting, and it's all your fault," Lisa snarled at me.

My fingers clenched into fists at my side. I didn't realize how hard I was squeezing them until my nails dug into my skin, causing sharp pain to shoot through my hands.

But I barely noticed, because my vision had gone red and splotchy with anger.

What was Lisa's problem? Why couldn't she just leave me alone? Even if she was stressed out, she was being really unfair about it, taking it out on me. It wasn't like I was the one who'd decided she had to take the SAT exam.

I longed to fling a retort at Lisa, but I managed to stop myself by biting down on my tongue. The last time I'd shouted something in the heat of the moment without thinking, I'd betrayed my sister's secret. Maybe I'd already done enough damage.

By the time our Honda Civic pulled into the high school driveway, Mama and Baba were having an all-out shouting fest. Lisa was saying something to me, too—no doubt something mean and rude again—but I couldn't even hear over the noise of our parents' fight.

"PLEASE, CAN EVERYONE STOP YELLING?" I finally burst out. I wanted to cry, but I forced the tears back. If I started bawling like a baby, Lisa would have a field day with it. The last thing I wanted was to give my sister even more ammo. "It's my recital, okay? I've been working on this for months. Please, just stop fighting for a little bit."

My words must've gotten through to my parents even over their shouting, because they exchanged a guilty look and then turned back to me.

"You *have* been working hard," Mama said. "No more fighting today from anyone. Is that clear?"

"We don't want all the money for your piano lessons and

registration for the recital to go to waste," concurred Baba. I resisted the urge to roll my eyes. Of course my father had found a way to rope money into the discussion.

Lisa sniffed and turned away to glare out the window, but she didn't say anything else to argue the point. I took a deep breath.

Miraculously, my family kept their word. We were so pleasant to the families of the other performers, and to each other, that I knew none of us had forgotten our fights but were merely squashing down any ill will to keep up a pleasant public image. It was all about miàn zi, or saving face.

It turned out that I wasn't the only one in the family who was performing that day. Almost all the members of Mama's circle of suburban mom friends, a.k.a. the Chinese aunties, were there to support their kids in the recital. The parents were the real stars of the piano performance, if you asked me.

There was Mrs. Wen, standing beside Mr. Wen and their ten-year-old genius son, Sam. Mrs. Chu, who was chasing down her eight-year-old daughter, Grace. Mrs. Qiao, who had her hands resting on the heads of her sixteen-year-old twins, Mitchell and Millie. And, of course, there was Mrs. Zuo, who was next to a bored-looking David in a black suit with a blue bow tie. Allison Tan was there with her parents, too, and she gave me a small wave from across the room.

The aunties were currently engaged in their favorite get-together activity: humblebragging about their kids' amazing accomplishments until they were blue in the face. The way my parents compared Lisa and me was a warm-up act next to how the aunties and uncles compared their children.

"Sam here just achieved a near-perfect score on his practice SAT, but, of course, that's nothing compared to *your* Mitchell's perfect score, Mrs. Qiao—"

"Grace won the top prize in the art competition at her school, but your Amy would draw circles around her—"

When I heard *my* name being mentioned, I knew it was time to excuse myself to the bathroom. I hated when the adults talked about me like I wasn't even there.

On the way to the bathroom, I passed by a very long table full of refreshments: fancy adult food like meats and cheeses and grapes, but also some fun food like samosas and Asian treats. There were even pineapple cakes and White Rabbit candies.

I picked up one of the pineapple cakes and bit into it. Mmmm. Flaky, but also tender and chewy, with a thick, jam-like pineapple filling. It was gone all too soon.

Okay, maybe I'd have just *one* more pineapple cake.

"Yo, Winnie."

I turned around with a mouthful of pineapple cake and nearly choked on the food. It was David. Joe, looking as grumpy and unpleasant as ever, was floating at his shoulder.

David gave me a concerned look as I tried to stop coughing.

"Oh—h-hey," I managed to splutter.

"Clumsy as ever, I see," quipped Joe. I glared. He went cross-eyed and stuck his tongue out at me. For a spirit who was as old as a dinosaur, Joe sure was immature.

"Need a sip?" David raised his cup of water toward me.

I took it and gulped it down, and the coughing finally subsided. "Don't sneak up on me like that, David," I accused, wiping the water off my lips with the back of my hand. "You almost gave me a heart attack."

"Not much of a superhero, are you?"

"Keep your voice down. That's supposed to be top secret," I hissed. I scanned the groups of people closest to us, but thankfully none of them seemed to have any interest in what David and I were talking about. "Plus, when did I ever say I was a superhero?"

David leaned in super not-discreetly and said, "Have you given more thought to my proposal?"

It took me a moment to figure out what he meant by *proposal*. "Teaming up to fight evil spirits?" I shook my head. "My answer is still no. I'm surprised you're not too busy to be thinking about all this shaman stuff."

"Yeah, well, I'm good at prioritizing what's most *important*." David raised his eyebrows at me in a condescending way that I didn't like. The nerve of him. He heaved a weary sigh that sounded too heavy for a kid. "Look, at the very least, I think you should apologize to your grandmother. She's the only one who knows what she's doing. Without her, neither of us can do anything."

"It's not a good idea to pick a fight with your overspirit," said Joe with an admonishing look. "You're acting quite childish, to be frank."

"Well, I am a child," I pointed out.

He frowned, as though he hadn't considered that. "Oh. Right."

I chewed the edge of the empty plastic cup, guilt sinking in the pit of my stomach. "My grandmother hasn't come back from the spirit realm yet. I think . . . I think she's mad at me," I admitted. If Lao Lao was angry with me, I deserved it. I was currently the front-runner for the Worst Granddaughter Ever award.

"Have you tried telepathically communicating with her? Just concentrate real hard, like this." Joe pressed his fingers to his temples and squeezed his eyes shut, his face scrunching up.

"Is that what I look like when I try to communicate with you?" David said in horror. He shuddered.

Joe opened his eyes and scowled at David. "My dear boy, you'd be fortunate to possess looks as good as mine one day."

David rolled his eyes and turned toward me, as if to say, *Can you believe this guy?* We smiled at each other. Then I stopped smiling when I remembered this was David.

"Winnie, did you bring any mooncakes with you?"

"Yes," I replied a little hesitantly. That crease between David's eyebrows was all too familiar. I recognized it as his "I have a brilliant idea" look. The fact that he was asking about the mooncakes was a clear indicator of which direction this conversation was going, and I wasn't sure that I liked it.

Yeah, maybe I'd brought along the mooncakes *just in case* something happened. Maybe I'd brought them along because they comforted me, gave me a sense of peace. But maybe part of me had anticipated that we might have to battle pesky spirits. Maybe that part of me had even *wanted* this. I shoved the thought away before it could really take root.

"Can't you, like, use the mooncakes to summon your grandmother?" David was saying. "They were what brought her here, right? Or maybe we could take a trip to the Department of Supernatural Record-Keeping again. That cat lady might be able to help." David slid a glance over at Joe. "Joe, can't you track down her whereabouts? Check in with the Spirit Council or something?"

"I'd have to leave your side for a while," said Joe, raising an eyebrow. "It's quite a trip to the Spirit Council Headquarters. Gotta go up eight hundred and eighty-eight levels, you know."

"How long does that take?" I asked.

"An hour . . . give or take an hour."

"Wait," David said, looking confused as he counted on his fingers. "So that means it might take no time at all?"

"Depending on the traffic, yes."

"What kind of traffic could you possibly get into in midair?" I spluttered.

Joe glowered at me, as though answering such a question was beneath him. "The number of birds, and don't even get me started on the most *horrid* variety of flying insects. You wouldn't believe—" He closed his eyes and shuddered. Even though we were currently having an evil spirit emergency, I had to stifle a grin. I was pretty sure we'd just learned Emperor Joe's weakness—flying bugs. "A-anyway, never you mind! Time is money, young one."

"We've got time," David said. "All I'm doing is this piano recital anyway. I'll be fine."

The old spirit squinted at David with doubt. I expected him to say no, but then he sighed and shook his head. "All right. I'll go look around the Spirit Council Headquarters. Don't get into any trouble while I'm gone."

"Don't worry. Piano recitals are the most boring thing on earth," I reassured him. "Nothing ever happens. We'll be fine."

Joe shot us a look as if to say that we'd *better* be fine, and then he gathered his robes. He spun in the air and then vanished on the spot, leaving David and me alone.

"Okay, well, see you later," I said. All this talk of spirits was making me extra nervous, which was the last thing I needed before performing piano in front of an audience.

I made to move past David. He grabbed my arm. I tried to twist out of his grasp, but he held on tight. What the heck was his problem?

David's frown was full of frustration. "Maybe you're

comfortable just sitting back and letting some evil force destroy this town—"

"Nothing's being *destroyed*, David. Quit being so dramatic—"

"But I'm not. I'm going to prove myself worthy of joining the Shaman Task Force. And I won't let you—"

But I never got to find out what David wouldn't let me do. At that moment, the loud, screeching noise of microphone feedback interrupted us. David's grip on my wrist slackened, and I took the chance to dodge away from him and fling my hands over my ears.

"Welcome, welcome, everyone!" came the voice of our piano teacher, Mrs. Kotov. Then she promptly turned around and let out a loud sneeze that echoed throughout the auditorium. "Oh, pardon me." She sniffled. "It's quite chilly these days, isn't it? Anyway, we'll warm things up with this recital in a moment. First things first—has anyone seen a pair of false teeth lying around? Mr. Jung has lost his . . ."

As everyone began settling down, taking their food to their seats in the auditorium, I turned away from David. "I gotta go. You should go find your family, too."

I had a performance to put on. And nobody—not spirits and especially not David—was going to outshine me today.

CHAPTER SEVENTEEN

I followed the crowd, letting myself get pushed along as everyone hurried to their seats. Within moments, I spotted my family sitting up in the front left. It wasn't hard to find them. My parents were standing and waving wildly at me, like they were trying to hail down an airplane. And Lisa was sitting with her back to me, her head buried in her SAT prep workbook. All around me, there was excited murmuring, and some stifled sneezes and coughing as well. Dang, I really hoped we wouldn't all get each other sick at this recital.

"Winnie, where did you run off to?" Mama whispered as soon as I sat down next to Lisa. "I turned my back on you for two seconds, and then you were gone!"

I frowned. "I told you I went to the bathroom. Didn't you hear me?"

"Oh." My mother frowned, looking distracted. "Well, next time make *sure* I hear what you're—"

"Indoor voices please, everyone, so we can get the recital started," boomed Mrs. Kotov into the microphone. She shot Mama a pointed look. Mama, her cheeks turning red, whirled around and made a shushing motion with her finger at me, as though I'd been the one being loud.

Grown-ups. They act like such children sometimes.

"Thank you," Mrs. Kotov said once the auditorium was quiet, except for the occasional crying noises of a toddler in the back. "Welcome, students, to the annual piano recital! You've all worked so very hard this year and achieved magnificent results at the piano competition this summer. This recital is all about celebrating your music, and all that you've accomplished. I—I'm just so *proud* to call myself your teacher." She wiped a tear away from her eye. I heard a few sniffles from parents around me, including Mama.

Oh brother. Something told me Mrs. Kotov's sob-fest speech was going to last longer than all our performances put together.

After going on for several more minutes, my piano teacher finally said, "Anyway, that's enough babbling from me. This day is all about *you,* the students. Without further ado, I'll introduce our first performer: Janice Jung, Level One, performing Bach's Prelude in C Major!"

There was a round of applause for a tiny girl with black pigtails, who practically ran up to the piano to start playing. Unlike the way I'd been at her age, Janice seemed to have no hesitation about being in the spotlight at *all.*

The familiar butterflies formed in my stomach. I couldn't help it. I always got super nervous about performing in front of others, no matter how many times I'd done it. Once I got up to the piano, I'd be fine, but the waiting, the anticipation, was always the worst part.

Janice made a few mistakes here and there but otherwise played the song perfectly. I'd played the Prelude in C Major a few years ago, so I still remembered the song, and I recognized when it was coming to an end.

Sweat formed on my palms, and I reminded myself to take deep, steady breaths, in and out. But somehow, no matter how deeply I breathed in the air, I couldn't shake off the horrible swooping sensation in my gut. Janice finished and took a bow, to enthusiastic applause from the audience. My hands were clammy with cold sweat when I brought them together a couple of times.

"Next up—Winnie Zeng, Level Seven, performing Rachmaninov's Elégie."

That was my cue to go up to the stage. For a moment I sat frozen in my seat, unable to move my legs. *This is it.* My heart hammered against my chest. I tried my best not to freak out, which of course only made me freak out even more. If I messed up, all those hours practicing piano would go to waste, and my parents would be furious with me. I was nervous as heck, but I had to pull this off. I didn't have any other choice.

Mama turned to me, beaming, and Baba gave me a thumbs-up. Lisa looked up from her book to give me a tight smile, which vanished after a second, so quickly that I might have simply imagined it. I wanted more than anything for those smiles to stay on their faces. Hopefully, my performance would be up to my parents' standards.

I forced my legs to move, even though it felt like I was trying to walk on five-hundred-pound bags of jelly. My eyes focused on the piano bench as I headed for the stage. Those butterflies were still fluttering in my stomach, and my hands were cold and sweaty. In fact, my whole body was cold. The air-conditioning in this building was way too powerful.

When I sat down on the ice-cold bench and positioned my hands on the keys, it struck me that it wasn't just nerves getting to me this time. I knew this chilly sensation that was wrapping itself around my body—and *inside* my body.

An evil spirit was stirring. And unless I was mistaken—and my shaman senses were tingling, telling me I wasn't—this one was far more powerful than the previous two. This one was a class three spirit.

"Not now," I groaned, as though that might make the cold sensation go away. I couldn't believe this was happening, that an evil spirit was gathering its power right then and there as I was about to perform for the crowd—the biggest crowd I'd performed for so far, even if a considerable chunk of the audience was just the Chinese aunties. I couldn't believe that the spirit was ruining the performance I'd worked toward for months and sabotaging my chance to make Mama and Baba proud of me. Not to mention, the entire audience was now in danger, too. I had to protect them.

What had David and I just told Joe? That piano recitals

were the most boring thing on earth, and there would for *sure* be no spirits attempting to attack during the performance. Well, we'd been dead wrong about that. Oops.

Panicking, I made a split-second decision. I'd play my piece as planned, maybe speeding up the tempo just a tad. As soon as I'd finished and the audience was applauding for me, I'd dash off the stage, grab my backpack, and hunt down the spirit before it caused any real mayhem. I wasn't sure what I could do without Lao Lao by my side. Still, I had to do *something*.

My hands shook, but I forced my fingers to steady as I began to play. I'd had plenty of practice playing through nerves before. I tried not to think about the fact that those nerves had been more of the stage fright variety, and not the current evil-spirit-going-to-wreak-havoc-on-Groton variety.

Everyone knows that the more you try *not* to think about something, the more you end up thinking about it. So my mind raced a mile a minute. Sweat trickled down the back of my neck. After I finished this piece, how was I going to head off the evil spirit? I had to come up with a plan—now.

I'd only finished playing the opening stanzas of the Elégie when all heck broke loose. A scream rent the air behind me. Shocked, I fumbled the next stanza, playing all the wrong notes. More screams followed. I turned around.

The scream had come from Mrs. Kotov. Something was very, very wrong with her. Her body was shuddering, and her eyes had turned red. She chucked her microphone into the crowd, causing audience members to dive out of the way. The microphone cracked with a sickening thud against the back of an empty seat, which Mr. Qiao had deserted only moments before.

"ROOOOOOOOOOAR!" shouted Mrs. Kotov.

"Wh-what's wrong with her?" cried out one of the older pianist boys sitting near the front.

"What's wrong with *all* of them?" screamed the girl next to him, pointing at the crowd of parents who'd been sitting directly in front of Mrs. Kotov.

The parents had begun shaking and behaving in the same strange way as Mrs. Kotov. They picked up their chairs easily, as though they were featherlight, and began throwing them at other audience members. Within seconds, everyone was screaming and panicking.

I was frozen to the piano bench in horror. The last two spirits had only been able to possess one person at a time. Matt Zingerman. Principal Tang. How was this one managing to possess a whole crowd of adults now, bending them so easily to its will?

Lao Lao's previous warning rang in my ears now. She'd told me that class three spirits were different from the others. A shaman could only capture a class three spirit by calling its True Name and sealing it into its book. Otherwise, the spirit would only continue to grow stronger the longer it fed off the discord of humans in our town.

But I hadn't taken Lao Lao seriously enough. And now my grandmother wasn't here to help me. David's overspirit wasn't here, either, because he'd gone looking for Lao Lao. All these people were going to pay the consequences for my stupidity—if I didn't do something about it, and quick.

Lao Lao wasn't here this time, so I couldn't access her powers. But I'd at least had the foresight to bring my magic mooncakes.

The problem was that the mooncakes were currently sitting in my Pusheen backpack, which was under a broken chair in the front row. Luckily, the possessed adults hadn't seen the backpack yet, but it was only a matter of time before one of them tossed it away.

The second problem was that Mrs. Kotov was advancing on me with the broken leg of a chair, brandishing it like a sword.

"You're in for it now, shaman," she said in a cruel, distorted voice that sounded nothing like her usually ethereal one.

I looked around wildly but spotted no weapon that I could defend myself with. Worse—Mrs. Chu, whose glasses had been knocked askew but who didn't seem to notice or care, was advancing on me from the other direction. She wielded a large, transparent plastic platter in her hands, which she'd swiped off the refreshment table.

There was no other option. I was going to have to make a break for it and hope both of them were too slow to catch me. Given that my hundred-meter-dash record was an unimpressive eighteen seconds, the odds weren't in my favor.

Then, out of nowhere, someone rushed at Mrs. Kotov.

The piano teacher fell with a shriek, and tripped Mrs. Chu in the process. Both women went tumbling to the floor of the stage.

David jumped up from the mess of tangled limbs and yelled, "Run, Winnie!"

I was way ahead of him. I sprinted past David with a breathless "Thanks!" and made a beeline straight for my backpack. As soon as I grabbed it, I dove out of the way as another possessed parent took a swipe at me. Then I hit the ground running.

Dang, I am never going to slack off in gym class ever again, I promised myself as a painful stitch formed in my side.

After sprinting to the back of the auditorium, I managed to catch my breath for a few seconds. One quick scan of the space showed me that everyone who hadn't been possessed had made it out safely. David was sprinting his way up the aisle, dodging possessed people left and right. Within moments, he braked to a stop in front of me.

"So—glad—my dad always made me watch—Chinese wǔ xiá movies," David said with a huge breath of relief.

I grabbed my mooncakes out of the ziplock bag and handed three to David, keeping the remaining three to myself. "Let's take care of this spirit," I said.

"Joe is never going to let me hear the end of this," David sighed. "Why'd a spirit have to attack the *moment* I told my overspirit to leave?"

"It's too late for regrets now. Just fight for your life!" Breaking the mooncakes into smaller pieces, I chucked them at the remaining adults—five of them. David and I had gotten pretty good at aiming by now. The mooncakes bounced off the possessed adults, burning their skin. Each time a piece of mooncake hit them, the adults would let out a ghastly wail of pain, like they were being buried or boiled alive, and then collapse to the ground. The silvery-white substance of the class three spirit floated high above their bodies and then swept out of the room before we could chase it.

Not that we *could* do anything even if we did give chase. David and I hadn't unlocked the ability to know True Names yet.

Within minutes, it was all over. David and I fell to the floor, like all the adults had moments before.

"That . . . was . . . wild," David panted, wiping sweat off his forehead. His glasses had fallen down his nose, and he pushed them up.

The stitch in my side still throbbed painfully. Yeah, I really needed to work harder in gym class from now on. When I'd finally caught my breath, I muttered, "I can't believe that just happened."

"Can't you?"

I glanced up, startled. David's voice sounded flat and unsympathetic. Angry, even. Bewildered, I said, "I mean . . . I just didn't think, like, another spirit would attack again so soon. And not *here*. I figured . . ."

"You figured you could just keep ignoring your shaman duties until it became convenient for you?"

"I . . . that's not what I . . ." I blinked, stunned at the harsh words. David continued to glare at me. He'd probably been holding back these thoughts for a while.

"What, you figured evil would sit around waiting until you had an opening in your schedule to deal with it?" If David's words could have taken physical form, they would have been like hot, boiling lava, pouring out of his mouth and scalding me.

I swallowed back a lump in my throat. The way David was twisting the situation was unfair, but no good defense came to mind. "It's not like that, David. I—I'm trying. I really am. It's not that I don't care about fighting evil. I just—I just have a lot to deal with, all right?" I had to make my parents proud. I had to make the spirit of my grandmother proud. And I had to save the world, too? Why didn't anyone else, even David, realize that this was too much for one eleven-year-old to handle?

"So do I, but I think this is more important than getting good grades or practicing piano," snorted David, gazing at me with a look that I'd never seen on him before. I'd endured his eye rolls, annoyance, and even all-out anger, but this was one of pure disgust. "You only care about your shaman duties when the evil spirits are directly hurting *you*, don't you? Some hero *you* are."

I couldn't think of a decent comeback. David was right. I wasn't hero quality—at all.

"I never said I was a hero," I finally said, but it sounded pathetic even to my ears.

David opened his mouth to retort but was interrupted by the sound of a *pop!* Behind him, Joe emerged out of nowhere. "Sorry, kiddo, but I checked with the Spirit Council and couldn't find your grandmother anywh—*Whoa.* What happened?" The spirit gawked and spun around to take in our surroundings.

"A spirit attacked," David said glumly. "We think it was a class three spirit this time."

Joe almost fell out of the air, which is to say he tumbled backward in shock. "*What?* The class three spirit that's been sending other spirits after you?"

David and I shrugged, not looking at each other.

"I was gone for all of thirty minutes," groaned Joe, smacking himself on the forehead so hard that his hat nearly fell off. "You said piano recitals are boring!"

"They are! Usually the most exciting thing is one of the older audience members losing their dentures," David protested.

"Okay, never mind, never mind. Where did the spirit go?" demanded Joe. David and I only shrugged, which irked him even more, judging by the sour expression on his face. "Well, what are you standing around for? Time to chase after it!"

"Winnie's going to stay behind and work on *more important things,*" David said, spitting out the last three words. "You and I are alone in tracking down this one, Joe."

"Oh. Is that so?" Joe gave me a look full of disappointment, and I had to glance down at my toes. The way they were staring at me made me feel like a coward. Well, I guess I *was* a coward. "It's not that I don't believe in our skills, David, but, you know, it would be a lot easier to take down this class three spirit if Winnie and her grandmother teamed up with us. Much as I hate to admit it, that old hag is quite powerful," grumbled Joe.

Guilt shot through me. I looked away from Joe and David and stayed silent. I didn't know what I could say. They were right. And I'd messed up by chasing Lao Lao away. Even if I did want to team up with Joe and David to fight the class three spirit, I couldn't do it without Lao Lao by my side. And I had no idea where my grandmother had gone.

"Nah, we don't need Winnie." David's voice came out ice cold.

"Well, David, I have a few centuries of shaman training on you, and I'm fairly certain that we *do* actually need Winnie," Joe said. "That's why the Spirit Council assigned two shamans and overspirits to Groton—"

"Whatever, we'll figure it out. C'mon, let's go." David shook his head, stood up, and wordlessly turned on his heel. He stormed out of the auditorium, with Joe behind him. A piece of toilet paper trailed from the bottom of David's shoe and then whipped out of sight.

CHAPTER EIGHTEEN

Stupid David.

I spent most of the day too angry to do homework. I knew I'd regret putting it off until later, but I didn't care. I'd just battled a very strong and angry spirit. That meant I'd earned a break.

Plus, David's parting words had put me in a foul mood. The way he'd spoken to and glared at me had been so condescending. What did he know about my life, anyway? Who'd made *him* the boss of being a shaman?

The worst part was, I couldn't vent to anyone about the piano recital fiasco. The adults had no memories of the spirits, and the story that went around was that a wild animal had gotten into the auditorium and caused mayhem. Nobody knew the truth about what was happening in Groton, and the real reason I was stressed—that an evil spirit capable of great damage was on the loose.

My gaze fell upon Jade, who was still barely eating anything. She definitely looked thinner than she'd been before Lao Lao had stopped talking to me and disappeared.

"You're the only one who isn't mad at me, Jade," I mumbled. "You're my only friend in this world."

Jade didn't say anything. Of course not. It wasn't like the spirit of my grandmother was about to talk to me through her.

And after all, Jade was a normal, nonspeaking rabbit.

After trying and failing to concentrate on my homework, I finally caved and texted David. Even if we'd parted on bad terms, part of me still worried about him and Joe. I wanted to know if they'd managed to capture the rogue spirit.

Winnie: Hey how did the spirit-hunting go?

David: 👎 Can't track it down and capture it without knowing its True Name.

Winnie: Oh . . . I guess.

David: Have you heard from your grandmother?

Winnie: No . . . 😟 I tried contacting her too

David: Like how Joe showed you lol?

Winnie: Yeah I made the weird face and everything 😖

David: Imma tell him what you said

Winnie: Omg pls don't

David: Too late

Winnie: DAVID

David: I'm jk, but I do hope your grandmother returns soon. We'll keep looking too. Joe's getting worried

After reading David's messages, I laid my head on my textbook. Suddenly, it felt like the weight of the world was sitting on my shoulders.

My grandmother was missing, and I couldn't exactly tell anyone besides David, because she was, well, dead. No way could I file a missing person report with the police—they'd yell at me for wasting their time. And here I was, trying to focus on homework, when deep down I really wanted to find Lao Lao.

By Sunday afternoon, I still hadn't managed to contact Lao Lao, nor had she returned. I'd finished most of my

homework. The biggest task left to tackle was baking desserts for the sixth-grade bake sale the next day, the same day as the Mid-Autumn Festival.

I couldn't believe that just a couple of weeks earlier, making sure that my class won the bake sale competition had been one of my biggest concerns. Now nobody was speaking to me except for David, but that wasn't really a flex. It was enough to put any girl in a very bad mood. And being in a very bad mood meant I did not want to bake anything, which was why I'd been putting off this task all weekend.

By late afternoon, I realized I couldn't put it off any longer. I headed downstairs and made a beeline for the kitchen. There wasn't much time left, so I wanted to whip up something simple and quick for the bake sale—maybe chocolate chip cookies or brownies. Something super easy. And definitely no mooncakes, because I didn't need to summon any more spirits, good or bad.

Someone was already in the kitchen. Mama. She was humming to herself and stirring a huge pot on the stove with a wooden spatula. I lifted my nose into the air and caught a whiff of something savory.

"We're having egg-and-tomato stew for dinner tonight," Mama said, beaming at me. Then her expression changed when she caught the look on my face. "Is something wrong, Winnie?"

"Nothing," I said quickly. This wasn't anything Mama could help me with. Not unless I let her in on all the magical happenings in our town lately. Yeah, like *that* was gonna happen.

I grabbed the nearest dessert cookbook out of the cabinet and flipped through the pages. If this cookbook turned out to be magical, too, I was going to lose it.

"What're you making?" Mama pressed.

I sighed, resigning myself to the fact that my mother was determined to nose around here. "Brownies," I decided on the spot. "For a bake sale at school. It's tomorrow."

"Want me to help you? I've just finished with the stew."

"Sure," I found myself saying. My spirits lifted at the thought of baking with Mama. Some of my happiest times had been in this kitchen whipping up something tasty with my mother, after all.

I got out all the ingredients I needed for the brownie batter: flour, eggs, milk, cacao powder, baking powder, sugar, vanilla extract, and salt. By the time I'd piled everything onto the kitchen island, Mama had already gotten out the measuring cups and mixing bowls and preheated the oven. We made the *best* baking duo, if I did say so myself.

"Why don't we make red bean brownies?" Mama suggested. She held up a bag of red bean paste. "We still have some red bean left over, and I don't want it to go to waste."

I hesitated, even though I loved red bean brownies. "My classmates might not like that." The image of Jessamyn's, Tracy's, and Kim's horrified expressions at my lunch rose in my mind. I was certain those three would have some rude things to say about red bean paste. Maybe that beans were gross or something.

"Why wouldn't they like red bean brownies? This is one of the family's best recipes." My mother's expression was filled with genuine surprise. She probably had no clue what some kids who weren't Chinese American thought of our food. "If they've never had these brownies before, now is the perfect time for them to try."

"You just want to get rid of the red bean paste, don't you?"

"I won't let this bag go to waste," Mama said stubbornly.

Some people might say I was stubborn, but I was nothing compared to Mama. She was determined. And red bean brownies *were* more delicious than regular brownies, after all.

"Maybe we can do half regular brownies and half red bean brownies," I suggested.

Mama agreed, and inwardly I sighed in relief. Quickly, we got down to business whipping up the brownies. We fell into a comfortable rhythm, with Mama passing me the ingredients and me mixing them together. The stress of everything that had happened lately melted away with the chocolate.

"How come you never became a chef, Mama?" I asked as I stirred the ingredients together.

"You have flour on your nose," my mother said, leaning over and wiping off a spot on my nose.

"Oh. Oops." When a silence fell between us again, I pressed, "I know Lao Lao is—I mean, was—the owner of a restaurant in Shanghai. Didn't you want to take it over for her?"

"Being a chef wasn't realistic for me," Mama said with a wistful look in her eye. "When your father and I came here from China, we gave up our dreams, you know. We wanted to have a better life. To give you and Lisa a better life." A small, sad smile stretched across her face, emphasizing the wrinkles under her eyes. "Your Lao Lao did hope for me to take over her restaurant. I believe that I . . . I may have broken her heart by choosing to leave Shanghai for America."

"Wow." I gulped. If Lao Lao ever decided to come back to the human world and speak to me again, I was definitely going to ask her about that. "But you're glad that you came here, right?"

"I am. I had to pursue what was most important to me, even if that meant letting down your Lao Lao. And what was important to me was raising a family in the land of plenty."

I had to pursue what was most important to me. Mama's words struck me as eerily similar to David's from yesterday, and guilt bubbled up inside me at the thought of how *that* conversation had gone.

"Mama," I said slowly, "I have a question."

"Yes?"

"Hypothetically speaking . . ." I licked my lips, which had gotten dry. "Hypothetically speaking, if you had to make a difficult choice between doing something important to you that would help—um—a lot of people, or doing something that would make just a couple of people happy . . . but not yourself . . ." I gulped. "What would you do?"

Mama smiled at me. I noticed there was flour on her face, too. It made her look mischievous. "I think you already know the answer to that, Winnie."

I opened my mouth to retort that that wasn't an answer, but my voice faltered. The realization hit me. Maybe I *did* already know the answer to that. Maybe I'd known it all along, even if I'd tried to deny it.

Making Mama and Baba happy was important to me, but so was being true to myself. So was having the chance of a lifetime, to be a hero and save my town.

Maybe getting my parents' approval wasn't totally worth what I was giving up—especially not if it meant coming at the cost of Lisa's trust. I'd learned that the hard way.

"Now let's get these brownies into the oven," Mama said, humming to herself as she lifted the tray off the counter and into the warm heat of the oven. I shivered in anticipation, already smelling the delicious chocolaty-ness in the air.

And by the time the brownies were ready to take out of the oven, I'd made up my mind. I knew exactly what I was going to do.

I just hoped my grandmother would hurry up and come back so I could have a chance to make things right.

I grabbed a couple of brownies to, *ahem,* taste-test them. The rest I placed into food containers, ready to take to school the next day. On my way back upstairs, I passed by the living room. Lisa was staring at the TV, glassy-eyed.

She'd wrapped a huge blanket around her and was holding a tissue box. The sounds from the TV were punctuated with Lisa's loud sniffles.

On the screen, the mayor of Groton, Mayor Greene, was speaking to the local news anchor, Shirley James. People really liked Shirley—or at least they liked cracking Dad jokes like "*Shirley* not!" whenever she reported bad news. In tiny, boring towns like Groton, that was the sort of thing that passed for entertainment.

Just then, Shirley was reporting more bad weather. It had been stormy for a couple of weeks straight, and the next week was looking to be even stormier, which Shirley said was due to the cold front coming in from the East Coast. That explanation made sense, given that this fall had already been chillier than autumns in years past.

"Bundle up in those cardigans and sweaters, and stock up on those tissue boxes. It's shaping up to be a cold, gloomy fall for Groton," said Shirley.

"*Shirley* not!" cried Mayor Greene. Then he cracked up at his own joke. Shirley stood stone-faced. The mayor's laughter trailed off.

Lisa cringed. "God, I can't wait to graduate from high school and get out of this town." Privately, I agreed. Then Lisa let out another honking sound as she blew her nose.

"It's true that Groton has been hit with some exceptionally bad weather lately, though, and fall has just begun," continued the mayor. He straightened his navy-blue suit jacket and dabbed his sweaty bald head with a white handkerchief.

"There's been a bit of a gloom in this town, but chin up! There are lots of great activities coming down the pipeline. Groton will, of course, continue with all planned fall festivities, like the local apple-picking contest, haunted houses, corn mazes . . ."

"Unfortunately, it seems as though this cold front has also been accompanied by technology issues throughout the city," said Shirley. "Frozen pipes, power outages—we'll likely be seeing more of those as we head into a very cold winter, unless the weather changes drastically."

"That is *Shirley* concerning," said the mayor.

A vein jumped in Shirley's forehead.

Mayor Greene continued hastily, "Do take precautions, citizens of Groton. A guide to navigating troubling weather is available on our city website, and—"

Lisa turned off the TV. She turned and then blinked in surprise when she saw me. "How long have you been standing there?"

I startled, like I'd been caught doing something wrong. "Um . . ."

"Never mind." My sister shook her head and sighed. She stared down at her nails. Just as I was about to leave, she said, "Since you're here, I might as well tell you I broke up with Matt."

"Oh." Why was Lisa confiding in me, out of the blue? Then I realized. "Did you break things off because Mama and Baba found out about your relationship?"

"No, not really." Lisa snorted. "I mean, if it were a matter of what our parents thought, I'd keep dating him just to make them mad."

That sounded like a very Lisa thing to do.

My sister shrugged. "But I realized he wasn't that great of a guy." The icy tone of her voice told me not to press further, so I didn't. "So, yeah. I just wanted you to know, since you did cover for me a lot when he was here. Even if you still blabbed to our parents."

Leave it to my older sister to end on another jab. I could tell she was trying, though. This was the most Lisa had told me about her personal life in, like, years. "You'll find someone better," I said.

"Yeah, and when I do, you'd *better* keep it a secret. Got it?"

I nodded. I wasn't about to cross Lisa twice. I had a feeling that all the shaman powers in the world couldn't protect me from her wrath if I did. "Lisa, I . . . I'm sorry. You know, I wasn't planning to tell our parents about—about—"

She cut me off with a wave of her hand. "It's okay. It's on me, really. I've been under a ton of stress lately, and I just . . . took it out on you. I'm sorry."

I hadn't expected Lisa to apologize to me. She could hardly look me in the eye, and her shoulders were hunched over in guilt. "It's okay. I know you've had to deal with SATs and stuff."

"It's just . . ." My sister bit her lip, as though unsure of her next words. Then she sighed. "Everything seems to come to you so easily, Winnie. You're so good at school and piano. You're, like, Chinese parents' dream child."

Lisa's words shocked me. I blinked. "What are you talking about? Mama and Baba are always saying I have to be better at those things. You know how they are, always bringing up David." Just the thought brought a scowl to my face.

"Yeah, but that's because they're telling you how you can improve even further. You're already doing great." Her eyes narrowed. "You know that, right? Sometimes I get the feeling you don't even register how talented you are." With a serious expression, Lisa mumbled, "You're the golden kid." I heard the unspoken words. *Not me.*

For a moment, I was speechless. I'd always been so busy chasing David's shadow that it had never occurred to me that someone else—my older sister—had been chasing *mine.*

"Well, I . . . I can't play softball," I blurted out. "Not like you. I can't play any sports, actually."

"I know," Lisa said. It should've stung, but I couldn't even get annoyed, because it was true. Winnie Zeng and athletics did *not* mix. "But our parents don't care about that. They just care about our grades and piano. It's all they talk about with their friends." My sister rolled her eyes. Her next words came out all in a rush, as though she couldn't get them out fast enough. "I guess I . . . I wish piano and school could come easily to me, too. I haven't been the nicest sister to you. I'm sorry."

There wasn't much I could say to that, because Lisa was right. She hadn't been very nice to me for a few years now.

"I haven't been the best sister, either," I admitted. "I'll be better at keeping your secrets from now on."

Lisa gave me a small smile, which I returned. For a moment, as the silence stretched on, it felt like the huge gap between us had shrunk just a little.

Then Lisa broke the silence by blowing her nose loudly. "Geez. This cold is getting bad," she muttered.

"Want a red bean brownie?" I blurted, holding out one of the treats I'd baked.

Lisa raised her eyebrow. "I don't eat chocolate anymore. You know that." Then she paused and, after a moment, held out her hand. "Well, I do need some extra fuel for my next SAT practice exam. Maybe just this *one* time."

With a grin, I handed over the brownie.

CHAPTER NINETEEN

The next day I woke up fully determined. Nothing could stop me. Not the snooze button on my alarm. Not even the annoyed look Lisa gave me over her Frosted Flakes, which told me that we weren't going to be BFFs now just because I'd given her a red bean brownie.

Nothing would get me down today.

At the top of my to-do list for the day: I had to help my class win the sixth-grade bake sale, and after that, I'd apologize to David—*barf*—and work with him to try to capture the class three spirit. With or without my grandmother, I had to save our town. I just hoped the spirit wouldn't come back to attack before we had the chance to regroup.

But first—the bake sale. Because the whole school was in full swing for the Fall Fair, students were excused from their morning classes to set up with their homerooms. The first thing I did when I got to school was take my brownies to Mrs. Payton's classroom.

Immediately, I spotted a huge pink-and-white pasteboard with A VERY SWEET WELCOME TO MRS. PAYTON'S CLASS'S

BAKE SALE written across it in big block letters with a black Sharpie. Below the words was a copy of our class photo, taken on the first day of school. The desks in the room had been rearranged to form several different stations, where students were setting up for the bake sale. There were Rice Krispies Treats, brownies, chocolate chip cookies, and lemon squares as far as the eye could see. My homeroom had pulled out all the stops. It seemed like everyone *really* wanted the extra credit.

"Ah, Winnie!" said Mrs. Payton, beaming at me as I turned on the spot, staring at the room. It was like I'd stepped into a totally different classroom. "What have you brought for the bake sale?"

"Brownies," I said, and then, after a moment of hesitation, added, "I brought twenty regular brownies, and twenty, um, red bean brownies."

"Red bean? That's very unique," said Mrs. Payton with a raised eyebrow.

"It's a family recipe." I took a deep breath to brace myself. Was my teacher going to make a comment on the red bean part?

"Well, I'm sure they're very delicious." To my relief, Mrs. Payton just smiled and handed me a piece of paper and a black marker. "Why don't you make a sign to advertise your different types of brownies, and put them out on the station? We're charging three dollars per dessert."

"Three dollars?" I yelped. Mama and Baba might have fainted if they'd heard we were charging people that much for one *piece* of a baked treat. I could practically hear Baba shouting about how many brownies he could make himself for the price of three dollars.

"Three dollars." Mrs. Payton didn't show even a trace of thinking these were the most expensive brownies in the history of ever. "That's the standard price Mr. Burnside and I agreed on. Well, I've got to go help your classmates, so I'll leave you to it, shall I? We'll be open for business in ten minutes!" Without waiting for an answer, she swept off toward Melissa Prince, who'd just walked into the classroom.

Whew. It wasn't even nine a.m. yet. I could already tell this was going to be a long day.

I finished setting up my sign and laying the brownies out on the table just in time for the bake sale to begin. Soon students and teachers trickled into the classroom, mostly from the seventh and eighth grades. Since the sixth-grade bake sale competition was the first activity of the day, it seemed like a lot of kids were trying to eat dessert for breakfast. Well, I was pretty sure what Mama's thoughts on *that* would be. But we were raising money for a good cause, so I guessed it was fine just this one time. Probably.

I waited nervously for the first wave of customers to make their way around the classroom. When two blond eighth-grade girls stepped up to my desk with curiosity, I crossed my fingers behind my back and hoped for the best. They'd probably never tasted red bean brownies before, so I had to really sell them.

"Red bean brownies?" asked the taller girl after reading my sign. She tilted her head to the side. "What's red bean?"

"Um, it's red bean paste," I said. "Red bean paste is . . . is like . . ." My mouth dried as I struggled to describe it. How was I supposed to describe a dessert that I'd grown up eating, that was as normal to me as chocolate chip cookies were to lots of other kids? "Um, well, it's pretty sweet, but not *too* sweet. And the consistency is thick, since it's a paste. It's kind of fudgy? Uh . . ."

The girls exchanged looks. I had no idea if I'd sold them on the red bean brownies or not, but my gut was leaning toward *not*. I had a sickening feeling that we were headed for an unpleasant scene.

Then the taller girl surprised me by saying, "I'll take one."

"Are you sure?" her friend whispered.

"Course I'm sure. I'm in the mood to try something new." She reached into her little pink crossbody bag and pulled out three dollars.

My first customer. I resisted the urge to jump and whoop for joy, which definitely would've scared these girls off. My heart did a little tumble of happiness. "Here you go." I handed her one of the ziplock baggies. She gave me her money, which I placed on the seat behind me.

The taller girl opened the bag eagerly but was interrupted by a snort behind her. My gaze fell upon a trio who had just come up to my desk, and my stomach dropped to the floor as I recognized who they were. Allison's swim teammates: Jessamyn, Tracy, and Kim. The girls who'd made fun of my food on the first day of school.

My stomach clenched. Uh-oh. Now we were *actually* headed for Lunchbox Moment: The Sequel.

"Red bean brownies?" said Jessamyn, a sneer twisting her otherwise pretty features. "Ew. That's so gross. Who puts beans in dessert?"

Tracy didn't say anything to agree with Jessamyn, but she didn't say anything against her, either. Kim stuffed her fist into her mouth as though to hide her giggling.

The two eighth-grade girls edged away, but not before I saw the girl who'd bought the brownie suddenly give her bag a wary look, as though it had done something to offend her.

My cheeks flamed. Jessamyn hadn't bothered keeping her voice down, which meant some of my classmates and the customers had glanced over at my station in curiosity. I had to say something. I had to stand up to Jessamyn and her complete lack of appreciation for good food.

The old Winnie never would have had the courage. But the new Winnie was different. The new Winnie was supposed to be hero.

Maybe heroes didn't have to always do big, flashy things, like fly through the sky with their capes billowing behind them, on their way to save the city. Maybe heroes could stand up to their own bullies first.

"Just because most Americans don't usually put beans

into dessert doesn't mean that people in other countries don't," I snapped. "Red bean paste is a really delicious treat in many Asian countries. You should stop making fun of something just because you don't understand it."

Jessamyn stared at me in shock, like she couldn't believe I'd dared to speak back to her. "Um, are you *lecturing* me? *You're* the one who brought this weird thing into school. Didn't it occur to you that you might get people *sick* because they've never eaten this before?" She glanced around her, as though waiting for someone to back her up, but no backup came. Even Tracy and Kim stared at their feet, staying silent.

"Oooh, I just tried your red bean brownie." All eyes turned to the girl who'd bought the dessert. She beamed at me, waving her half-eaten brownie in the air. "It's so yummy. I've never had anything like this before. I'm gonna buy another one!"

"I want one, too," her friend chimed in. The two of them practically shoved Jessamyn out of the way, holding out their money.

I couldn't resist the huge grin that formed on my face, stretching my lips from ear to ear. It grew wider still when I saw Jessamyn's ears turning bright red with anger. "Two more, coming right up."

Soon many other students and teachers, drawn by the commotion at my station, came over to check it out. Within half an hour, I'd sold every last red bean brownie. I couldn't believe it! We were *so* going to win this competition, and

David was going to be doing my Chinese school homework for a whole month.

And the best part was, people loved the red bean brownies. They loved the treats Mama and I had baked together.

At the end of the hour, Mrs. Payton swept by our stations to help us clean everything up. "Oh, well done, Winnie," she exclaimed when I handed over the huge stash of money my red bean brownies had earned. "You sold out! That's incredible. Mr. Pucey and Mrs. Anderson were raving about your brownies, by the way. They couldn't get enough, and they wanted me to ask you for the recipe! I have to confess that I'd like a copy for myself, too."

"I can get that, easy," I said eagerly. "I can get copies for the whole class, too, if you'd like me to."

"That would be *wonderful,* Winnie." Then Mrs. Payton's smile dropped slightly when she cast a look around at the class. I followed her gaze and realized that the room was empty. Everyone had gone on to the next scheduled activity: the seventh graders' pumpkin-carving contest. "Oh, silly me, I've lost track of the time. We'd better hurry up if we want to get to the seventh-grade hall!"

I followed Mrs. Payton out the door, still feeling like I was floating on cloud nine. I mean, everyone had adored the red bean brownies. They'd been a smash hit. I couldn't wait to tell Mama all about it later that night.

As soon as I left the classroom and stepped into the hall, an all-too-familiar cold chill swept through me, and the warm happiness abandoned me.

Oh no. This couldn't be happening. Not now.

Mrs. Payton hesitated, tilting her head down toward me, her eyebrows scrunched together with curiosity. "Winnie, did you feel that draft just now?"

"I—" Before I could say anything further, two girls stepped in front of us in the otherwise empty hallway. Tracy and Kim. Why couldn't they leave me alone?

"Girls, what are you doing hanging around here?" said Mrs. Payton, frowning at them. "You should be heading to the seventh-grade hall."

That horrible chilling sensation grew even icier in the pit of my stomach, and suddenly I realized that Tracy and Kim didn't look quite like . . . themselves. They were taller and more muscular. Their hair was longer and wild-looking, and their features were somehow distorted. They looked like teenage versions of themselves—but uglier.

Just like the times before, the lights in the hallway began flickering.

"What on earth?" Mrs. Payton said, frowning at the ceiling.

"They're possessed!" I gasped. "Mrs. Payton—run!"

I turned to dash away, my brain already scrambling to form a plan, and was surprised to see David hurtling down the hall toward us.

"Winnie! I felt—I knew—the class three spirit, it's here, isn't it? It—"

"David, GO BACK! IT ISN'T SAFE HERE!"

The mooncake. I still had a smushed mooncake in my

pocket. I grabbed it and split it in two, intending to give the other half to David.

Before I could pass the mooncake to David's outstretched fingers, something hard and heavy hit the back of my head. I felt the swooping sensation in my stomach that told me I was falling, and then everything went dark.

CHAPTER TWENTY

I was floating somewhere, surrounded by fluffy white clouds, and my mind was blissfully empty. The feeling was so rare that I almost couldn't recognize it. *Peace.* I was at peace. Wherever this was, I could stay here forever, without a care in the world. No piano recitals. No homework or tests. No pesky spirits. Nothing could bother me here.

As I floated along, I heard a distant voice, growing louder and louder. There was a small figure huddled over, and I was drifting closer to it. Irritation rose within me. Whoever it was, they were disturbing my peace.

"Go away," I said, but the volume of the voice rose. As I got nearer, I recognized the figure with a jolt—it was my grandmother. Relief flooded me. I'd finally found her. "Lao Lao!"

But the relief didn't last long. I realized that my grandmother looked to be in much worse shape than when I'd last seen her. Her tiny, frail figure was hunched over, and she had been bound with ropes. When her eyes met mine, I saw that they were wild and frantic.

"Winnie, you must *not* come," my grandmother said. "Whatever you do, don't give in to his demands."

"Whose demands? Lao Lao, are you okay?" My heart leapt with fear.

"*Him.* The class three spirit called the Gloomy One. I tried to go after him on my own, but I overestimated my abilities." More to herself than to me, Lao Lao said, "I—I fought him once myself, as a young shaman. I should've known he'd be back, and stronger than ever."

I didn't know what that meant, but I could tell from Lao Lao's frightened tone that whoever the Gloomy One was, he was not to be crossed.

Before I could press my grandmother for more information, a shadowy figure fell over her, blocking her from my view. The shadow was like dark gas and didn't take on any form that I could recognize.

And a terrible growl of a voice entered my head. *Give me the cookbook, or else this spirit disappears—for good.*

The thought of losing Lao Lao just when I'd finally gotten to know her was too much to bear, even though losing the cookbook would be painful, too. But I knew which was more important. A cookbook, even a magical one, could never be worth my grandmother. Even if it meant that losing the cookbook would cost me my shaman abilities.

Where should I meet you? I asked the shadowy figure.

The Department of Supernatural Record-Keeping. Be there within the hour—or else.

Before I could get in another word, everything around me vanished, and I jerked awake.

The bright light was rough and painful on my eyelids. Voices faded in and out of my hearing range, and I couldn't tell whether I was dreaming them.

". . . students and staff *frozen* . . . like something out of a movie . . ."

". . . not sure how the intruder got in . . ."

". . . a tall, buff, scary-looking man—no idea how he got in . . . a description? Er . . . sort of looked like Secret Service . . ."

I peeled open first my right eyelid, and then my left. Blinking furiously against the light, I took in my surroundings. White walls. A sink in the corner. A door that had been left slightly open, through which I could hear adults speaking in hushed tones. I was lying down on a cot, which meant I was in the nurse's office.

Pain throbbed in my right shoulder and knee, as though I'd fallen down on that side. Had I fallen down? I vaguely remembered feeling scared of being pursued by someone— or some*thing*—and a force shoving into me, and toppling over . . . and then that strange dream I'd had, where I'd been wandering in the clouds. Lao Lao had been there—she'd been kidnapped—and a dark figure had told me that I could get her back, if only I gave him the cookbook.

As the memory returned to me, I gasped. Right. I'd been with David, running down the hallway. I'd tried to hand him part of a mooncake, but an evil spirit must've gotten to us before I could. Somehow I'd ended up in the nurse's office—but where was David?

There were too many questions running through my head, getting all jumbled up. What stood out to me clearly was that I needed to get to the eighty-eighth floor of the Suntreader. I needed to get to the Department of Supernatural Record-Keeping and rescue my grandmother from the Gloomy One, no matter the cost.

I started to get up. Before I could swing both feet over the cot, the door opened fully. A disheveled Mrs. Payton stood there, her curly brown hair flying this way and that out of her ponytail. "Winnie! You're supposed to stay put until the nurse gets back here."

"Mrs. Payton?" I croaked, my voice rusty with disuse. I cleared my throat. "Wh-what's happened?"

My homeroom teacher opened her mouth, and then closed it tight, shaking her head. She seemed to struggle with herself for a moment. Then, once more, she opened her mouth. "I . . . I hesitate to share this with you, given your delicate state—"

"I'm *not* delicate," I protested. To show her, I stood up. Blood rushed to my head and made me dizzy, but I stood my ground with determination.

"—but seeing as they are your classmates and all . . . ," Mrs. Payton continued, more to herself than to me, "I suppose you should know. I—I don't even know how to explain this without sounding—I mean, the whole thing is ludicrous—but, well, a handful of students have somehow been frozen."

"Frozen?" I gasped.

"Frozen," my teacher confirmed tearfully. "It doesn't make sense, but some awful curse has fallen upon Groton. Something to do with the cold weather we've gotten lately. The security guards are still trying to figure out what's going on, but so far what they do know is that a—a man snuck into the school somehow, and right after that, a bunch of students were frozen. That man vanished before the guards could give chase. We've sent all the remaining students home for the day."

I gritted my teeth as Mrs. Payton pulled out a lacy pink handkerchief and sobbed into it. Even though my teacher didn't know all the details—or, indeed, any of the supernatural details—she'd conveyed the seriousness of the situation. The "man" must've been what the Gloomy One appeared like to everyone else, or maybe he'd possessed yet another person.

But I knew the truth.

I had to save them all. I had to rescue this town from the clutches of the Gloomy One. I had no clue how I was going to pull that off, but I did at least know the first step: get the heck out of here before the school nurse came back.

"You should rest, Winnie," said Mrs. Payton, still sniffling and dabbing at her eyes. "You've been through an ordeal, since you were almost attacked by that bad man, too.

We're trying to get this—this bizarre situation under control. You—*Winnie, what on earth are you doing?*"

"Sorry, Mrs. Payton!" I grabbed my backpack and swung it over my shoulder. Before the teacher could react, I dove past her and through the doorway, shutting the door behind me. Only the secretary was in the main office. It appeared that all the other staff members were still running around the school at the news of the latest victims of the "curse."

I had a clear path out of there, and I didn't waste a second. Dashing down the halls, I ignored teachers who shouted after me. Didn't stop to respond. Didn't even stop to think of a concrete plan. I did check my phone to see that I'd missed a couple of texts from David.

David: Hey just so you know, the class three spirit got into the building and froze a bunch of students. We all got sent home. Joe and I are on our way to head off this evil spirit at the Department, but we might need backup

Winnie: Are you there rn? I'm omw

There was no response to my text. David was fast with replies, so that didn't bode well. I sent another text and tried calling, but still no reply. My stomach sank, and I knew David was in trouble, too.

Good thing I'd decided to ride my bike instead of taking the bus this morning. Outside the school, I found my bike, the last one still on the rack, and quickly unlocked it. I pedaled home faster than I'd ever biked in my life.

"Get the cookbook, get the cookbook, get the cookbook," I kept muttering under my breath like a chant. I willed my legs to move faster.

By the time I'd reached my driveway and dismounted from the bike, my legs felt like they were on fire. I was going to have *awful* cramps tomorrow, and possibly for the rest of the year. But there wasn't a moment to waste worrying about that.

The front door was locked, which meant nobody was home. Good. I grabbed my key from my backpack, burst inside, and ran pell-mell up the stairs to my room. The remaining mooncakes I'd baked with Lao Lao the other day were where I'd left them—in a gallon-sized ziplock bag sitting on top of my desk. I opened the bag and ate one of the mooncakes for good measure. Instantly, warmth spread through my body, from the top of my head to my toes. I closed the bag and put it in my backpack to take to the bookstore.

Jade was where I'd last seen her in the morning, too, perched on the bed of pillows I'd made her. She was staring at me.

"Sorry, but you can't come with me," I said. "This mission is too dangerous." Jade's nose twitched, either to respond to what I'd said or just to get rid of a nose itch.

Jade couldn't come with me, but there was someone who could help me on this mission. Or, rather, he'd already gone off to the Department of Supernatural Record-Keeping, and I was the one who needed to aid *him*.

"I'm coming, David," I said to myself.

I grabbed the cookbook from my desk and shoved it into my backpack. Swinging the pack onto my shoulder, I turned around, preparing to dash out of my room again to head to the Department of Supernatural Record-Keeping.

But unfortunately, I hit my first obstacle as soon as I landed at the bottom of the steps.

"Going somewhere?"

Lisa stood in front of me with her arms folded across her chest, a cold look on her face.

CHAPTER TWENTY-ONE

I'd totally forgotten that Lisa had taken the day off from school because she was feeling sick. I wasn't sure which was more terrifying: facing down a full-fledged evil spirit or facing down my grumpy older sister. Seriously, if college didn't work out for Lisa, she could have a successful career as a demon.

But staring Lisa in the face, I rather thought I would prefer taking on the full-fledged class three spirit.

"H-hey, Lisa," I squeaked in a bad attempt at sounding casual. "Um . . . are you feeling any better?"

"No. In fact, I feel worse."

Oh, great. I had to say something, anything, to put her in a good mood. "Has anyone told you how amazing your, um, eyebrows look lately?"

"Cut the crap," Lisa snapped. "You're not going anywhere. You know you're supposed to be practicing piano and studying until Mama and Baba get home." Her eyebrows knit together. "Also, I heard that something weird went down at the middle school just now. Something about freezing? Anyway, you'd better stay home to be safe."

"But this is really, really important—"

"I don't want to hear it. I'm the one who's in charge right now, so you'd better listen to me."

It took all my remaining resolve to hold back the retorts I longed to hurl at Lisa. My hands shook and clenched into fists. I guess that moment we'd shared in the living room yesterday hadn't counted. Lisa was back to being her crabby, miserable self.

If my sister would just *listen* to me for once, she'd realize I wouldn't be doing this if it weren't a matter of life or death. For the umpteenth time, I wondered why I hadn't gotten a nice older sibling, like Allison's sister, Leah, who took her out shopping and to get froyo all the time. Why did my sister have to be the mean, old witch Yubaba from *Spirited Away,* trapped in a fourteen-year-old's body?

Spirited Away. That had been Lisa's favorite movie when we were younger. I wondered if it still was, or if she'd traded her love of Studio Ghibli for *The Simpsons,* like she'd traded her bubble tea for iced vanilla lattes.

Spirited Away was the story of a girl named Chihiro who's moving to a new home. Along the way, her family stumbles upon a resort that's meant for supernatural beings, and Chihiro's parents turn into pigs. That kind of derails their moving plans. And their getting-the-heck-outta-here plans. Anyway, point is, Chihiro gets into all sorts of trouble in this spirit world while rescuing her parents.

Just like Chihiro, now I had to rescue people from spirits.

Even if "people" were classmates who'd annoyed me at one point or another. Maybe I could try to appeal to Lisa by bringing up her favorite anime. It was worth a shot, at least. My backup plan was knocking her out, and I really didn't want to have to do that.

"Please," I said, throwing away my pride and putting on my best puppy-dog face for my sister. "I really, really have to do this."

Lisa's eyebrows rose at least half an inch. I wasn't exactly the politest little sister—and by that I mean I could recall only twice in my life when I'd ever said the word *please* to Lisa—so she must have realized something huge was going on. At last, she heaved a sigh. "What exactly are you doing? You can't expect me to let you go anywhere without explaining the full situation."

Every moment that slipped by was a precious moment wasted. I could practically see the way the Gloomy One was draining the warmth and happiness out of the whole city of Groton. Everything inside me felt chilly. Unless I was imagining it, the light in our hallway was flickering. I squinted at it. No, I definitely wasn't imagining it—the electricity in our house was starting to fail.

"What—what's happening?" Lisa's gaze followed mine up to the flickering light, and her eyes grew round.

"So you know how Chihiro from *Spirited Away* has to, like, outwit the evil witch Yubaba at the end in order to break the curse on her parents and rescue them?" I blurted out.

"Why the heck are you talking about anime now, of all things? I know how weird you are, but this is just—"

"The point is, I have to pull a Chihiro right now," I interrupted. *Pull a Chihiro.* Actually, I was pretty proud of coining that phrase—and I'd definitely be using it in the future, too. "You feel it, too, right? This chill all around us. And the electricity is starting to go out."

Lisa scoffed and waved a hand airily. "So Baba didn't pay the electric bill on time. Whatever. I'll just remind him when he gets home."

"No, Lisa. This problem isn't just confined to our house. If I don't go do this—*thing*—more people are going to get hurt." I held my breath, hoping against hope that Lisa wouldn't press me further. Just this one time, I hoped she would find the goodness buried in her heart—deep, *deep* in her heart—to let me go.

My older sister held my gaze for one, two, three heartbeats. Then she shook her head and heaved a weary sigh. Her face slackened with exhaustion, and she pressed a hand to her forehead. "Fine, go. Just—go. Do what you need to do. If you're not back by dinnertime, I'll tell Mama and Baba . . . something."

"Really? You're the best, Lisa!" I moved to hug my sister, but she stepped out of the way, looking alarmed.

"I'm still sick," Lisa explained.

We stood there awkwardly for a moment, before she put her arms around me and patted my shoulder. Then she backed away. "Don't go all sappy on me, now." But there was a small smile on Lisa's face. A second later, though, my sister swayed where she stood, and then stumbled backward and slouched onto the stairs.

"Lisa!" I shouted, lunging toward her.

"I—I'm fine." My sister swatted my hand away. "Just . . . had a light dizzy spell. I think I'll go lie down and . . ." She shuddered as a chill swept through the room.

And then, to my horror, Lisa's body began to turn blue. Icicles formed along her legs, climbing fast toward the top of her head. It all happened in moments.

"Lisa!" I shouted.

Her mouth struggled to form an O of surprise, but then her head was frozen, too. In a matter of moments, my sister had turned into a statue. The sight was too horrifying for me to fully register. I glanced away, taking a few deep, calming breaths.

All I knew was that if I didn't get out of here now, shaman powers or not, I'd probably be next to fall under the curse of the Gloomy One. If I didn't get out of here now, I'd lose my sister—forever.

"I'll save you, Lisa," I promised. I forced myself to look away from my sister's petrified gaze, turned around, and dashed out of the house.

CHAPTER TWENTY-TWO

As I pedaled around town, I saw marks of the Gloomy One's curse everywhere. People had been frozen gardening in front of their houses, walking their dogs, riding their bikes. At this point, I was certain that the only thing keeping me from freezing was the fact that I had shaman powers. The mooncakes kept me warm inside. But I didn't even know for how long those powers could protect me. So I pedaled hard, faster than I ever had in my life.

By the time I completed this mission, I was pretty sure I was going to hold the world record for Fastest Cyclist Ever. Like, those SoulCycle instructors had *nothing* on me.

First order of business after I finished with this rescue mission: I was going to invest in a cape. And learn how to fly. There was no way I could keep up my shaman duties on this puny, run-down bike. One more mission like this, and the poor thing would be toast.

As I drew closer to the Suntreader, the gloom grew around me. Even though it wasn't even noon yet, the sun disappeared behind gray clouds, and the sky steadily turned

235

a greenish-black color. The lights inside houses flickered, some of them going out entirely, plunging us into an ever-darkening atmosphere. It seemed like the spirit was sucking all the light out of Groton. I had to hurry.

I fought against the chilliness that was spreading within me. The mooncake had worn off. I'd never felt so cold in my life—nor did I think I ever would feel so cold again. Even as I tried to withstand it, a drowsy sensation overcame me. All I wanted to do was sleep. Was it really that big a deal if I let the spirit get away with freezing people, anyway? Would it be so bad being frozen forever?

Being frozen forever. The thought jolted me out of my stupor, snapping me back to reality just in time to narrowly avoid crashing into a stop sign. Going against all my instincts, I shouldered on through the cold and the exhaustion. The Gloomy One was manipulating the power in this town against me. He *wanted* me to fail before I even reached him.

I wouldn't let him win. I wouldn't let him have his way. I was going to save Lisa, as well as everyone else in this town.

When I finally rounded the corner and stopped my bike in front of the Suntreader, I saw that the Gloomy One had left a path of destruction in his wake. The front door of the bookstore had been left open, and the windows were shattered. There was no sign of David—or anyone else, for that matter.

Anger curled in my gut. Countless hours I'd spent on the other side of the window, browsing through manga, comics, and books. The nerve of this evil spirit, to destroy Groton's most beloved bookstore—and my sanctuary.

"Oh, you've done it now," I growled under my breath. Leaving my bike out in front of the store, I rolled up my sleeves. All thought of the danger that awaited me flew from my mind. The only thing that mattered right now was getting in there, rescuing Lao Lao, and giving this evil thing the beating of his life.

Before I could march through the doorway, I imagined what Lao Lao would say. She'd tell me to slow down and act with my head, not my heart. To keep my head steady and come up with a strategy for attack. After all, there were lives on the line. The logical part of me knew I had to exercise caution. There was still a lot I didn't know about shamanism, my powers, and the powers of the Gloomy One.

I ducked through the doorway, dodging a bit of dust that trickled down from the ceiling. Inside, the bookstore was a mess. It looked like a cyclone had come through, torn up the inside of the Suntreader, and vanished. Bookshelves had toppled over one another, like really big dominoes. The floor was littered with books, some of them so torn that they were irreparable, loose pages lying everywhere. The lights overhead had been shattered. They flickered on and off. I was afraid that at any moment, they would go out for good.

There were a few bookstore browsers, but I realized with a jolt that the Gloomy One's curse had already gotten to them. They'd been frozen in place. A teenage girl had been reaching for a comic book. An older woman held a romance novel and was frozen with her hand turning one of the pages. With a sinking sensation in my gut, I realized I recognized one of the frozen customers—it was Jessamyn from school. Even Mr. Stevens had been frozen behind the counter in a ducking position, an expression of horror on his face.

I forced myself to look away from the frozen people. I needed to track down the Gloomy One fast and get Lao Lao's help in restoring the life to these people.

I walked to the back of the store and toward the elevator, which appeared untouched. The elevator car came rattling a moment after I pressed the "up" button. Once I'd entered, I pressed the button for the eighty-eighth floor.

When I stepped out of the elevator, I saw that the Department of Supernatural Record-Keeping had been similarly ransacked. So much for the Paper Guard being made up of an elite crew. The members had either been knocked out or torn into pieces, and a couple had even folded over. I hoped they were just out of commission and not dead.

Xiao Mao the cat lady had been frozen as well, in the middle of typing something on her computer. Books had been flung about, and shelves had been toppled over. A few of the biting books had started chomping down on each other, causing a terrible mess of torn pages and sounds of biting and screeching.

At first, there appeared to be no signs of life among the wreckage aside from the biting books, but then I spotted movement in the shelves at the back, where a green mist had formed. David. It had to be David, and my grandmother. My heart raced as I tried to move as quietly as possible over the wreckage, quickly skirting the biting books.

As I drew closer to the green mist, the chill around and within me grew even colder. It felt as though all the warmth and light in the universe was being sucked away, into that dark corner of the Department of Supernatural Record-Keeping.

Shivering, I steeled myself. As much as I wanted to say "Psych!" and turn around and run away, I knew I couldn't back down. None of the Avengers would. Nor would any of the Sailor Scouts.

I needed to be like them—right here, right now. I had the cookbook, and in moments, I'd have my grandmother and David back by my side, too. Even if I couldn't feel Lao Lao's reassuring touch, her presence gave me strength all the time.

And then, as the green mist cleared away, I could clearly see what we were facing.

The Gloomy One took on the appearance of a huge, muscular man, as big as the Hulk, wearing brown pants but no shirt. He filled at least a third of the space in the whole room on his own. The class three spirit was glowing. It took me a second to realize what the source of the glowing was: light. The electricity in this bookstore was running from the overhead lightbulbs directly into the evil spirit's skin. And unless my eyes were playing tricks on me, with each passing moment, the spirit was swelling in size, growing from the light.

My glance flickered to the large forms lying against the wall, and I gasped. Those forms were David, Joe, and Lao Lao. They'd been bound by a glowing green rope that was made out of some supernatural substance, and all appeared to be unconscious.

"So," rumbled the evil spirit, "we meet officially, little shaman."

I quickly reached into my bag and pulled out a mooncake, holding it in front of me like a shield. "I—I am here to send you back to the spirit realm," I said, my voice entirely too squeaky for my liking. I grabbed Lao Lao's cookbook out of my backpack and held it in front of me, too, though I didn't know what the heck I was doing. "Evil spirit of—"

"Pitiful. This is the caliber of shaman that the Spirit Council chooses to protect humans these days? No wonder this world is going to the dogs," snarled the spirit. Electricity crackled through the air, causing another bookshelf to topple over. I dodged out of the way as a pile of books fell, right onto the spot where my left foot had been a second before. "At least in the olden days, shamans were respectable. It was an honor to best them. I miss those times. Defeating you wouldn't even count as a warm-up, little girl." The spirit drew himself to his full, admittedly impressive height, which looked to be anywhere from twelve to fifteen feet tall. "As much as I'd love to pass the time messing with you, I'm afraid I have a mission to complete. I need the essence of the moon. Now."

"I—I don't have the essence of the moon anymore," I said, trying to sound defiant rather than terrified. "I baked it into mooncakes."

"You *what?*" bellowed the spirit. "How dare you. That's my—my precious—you—" He turned away and took a deep breath, I assumed to compose himself, before turning toward me with renewed fury in his eyes. "Never mind. That cookbook—that's still useful to me. Hand over the cookbook, or I'll be ending your little friends' lives right before your eyes."

Panic surged inside me. I needed Lao Lao's power to help banish the spirit. I couldn't do this on my own. There was only one option left to me. Slowly, I held out the cookbook, and the Gloomy One's eyes filled with greed as he stretched his hands toward it.

No! It took a moment for me to realize that a voice had echoed in my head. The voice of my grandmother. She was unconscious, but somehow I could hear her voice. Maybe, it occurred to me, Lao Lao was pretending to be unconscious.

Lao Lao? Is that you?

Don't give him the cookbook, you silly girl. You'll be giving away a sacred power—a power that should only be used for good.

But what other choice do I have?

Your magic, Winnie. You remember our training to fuse our minds, right?

Yeah, but it didn't go so well.

Concentrate. You can do it. I know you can. Summon the happiest memories you have, and channel them into emotions. Let me in, and let my power become yours.

When the cookbook was only centimeters away from the Gloomy One, I snatched it back. "You're not taking anything," I snarled. My feet seemed to have a mind of their own, free from the complete terror I was feeling. I stepped forward, though my insides were screaming at me to run in the opposite direction.

The cookbook in my hand now felt as hot as my freshly baked mooncakes did. And somehow, that heat traveled from my fingertips, to my arm, to the inside of my body, chasing out the bitter chill of the gloom.

"You'll regret this choice," sneered the Gloomy One. "If you want to play, little shaman, then I'll give you a show. When I'm through with you and your friends, you'll have learned not to meddle in the spirits' affairs any longer."

"You don't scare me," I lied, hoping I sounded braver than I felt. "I have the spirit of my grandmother by my side."

The Gloomy One flickered his electrifying eyes toward my unconscious grandmother, appearing wholly unimpressed. "A little girl with a cookbook, and an old lady with no real powers to speak of who isn't awake. I'm quivering—*not*. I should be finished with you both *quite* soon."

Biting on my lip, I concentrated as hard as I could on summoning happy emotions. Harder than I'd concentrated on anything in my life. *Please help me rescue the others, Lao Lao. Lend me your power.*

I sensed a shift in the air, something that was different and much bigger than any power I'd been able to use in training before.

Now that our minds are finally aligned, all of my might is yours to use, little one. Let's finish this spirit. My grandmother's voice sounded loud and ethereal, echoing in my head.

My insides heated up, until I was sure I was burning— but not unpleasantly so. I looked down, and a blue fire had enveloped my body. I glanced at the Gloomy One. He'd thrown his arms up to shield his face, as though the sight of me was too brilliant and blinding.

This was True Sight. My heart pounded in a mad rhythm. I hardly dared to believe it, but I'd done it. I'd finally linked minds and emotions with my overspirit.

I'd never had particularly good eyesight, and now my vision had improved so much that it had to have shot right past 20/20. Maybe I was seeing 200/20. I could see the details within the wood of the bookshelves, not to mention every particle of dust on the floor.

I wouldn't let the spirit achieve his goal. I moved without hesitation, as though my body knew what to do better than my mind. I reached into my backpack and chucked one of the last magical mooncakes at the evil spirit. He dodged easily, but the mooncake managed to bounce off part of his muscled arm, creating a hissing, popping noise. The part of the skin the mooncake had hit burned bright red and then melted off.

For a moment, the Gloomy One and I both stared at his ruined bicep in stunned disbelief. "NOW YOU'VE DONE IT!" roared the spirit.

Far from being frightened by his threat, I was emboldened. The sight of his burned skin rejuvenated my spirits. I could do this. The Gloomy One was weakened. I simply had to open the cookbook, call his True Name, and banish him back to the spirit realm.

Hurry, Winnie, urged Lao Lao. *I don't know how much longer our connection can last.*

But before I could make a move, the overhead light-bulbs shattered.

CHAPTER TWENTY-THREE

Dust and debris flew everywhere. On reflex, I dove behind a fallen bookshelf, out of harm's way. The Gloomy One roared, and the whole building shook, including the floor. When the shakes finally stopped, I dared to look up from behind the bookshelf. Or, rather, I tried to look, but found I'd been plunged into sudden darkness. For a moment I could barely make out the huge outline of the Gloomy One as he lumbered through the debris, searching for something—probably me.

"Where are you hiding, shaman?" growled the spirit. "Not so brave now, are you? Come out and face me!"

This is your chance, Lao Lao said. *Get your friend while the spirit is looking away!*

I didn't need to be told twice. Though it was dark, my True Sight could see as well as if the room were perfectly illuminated. I'd just spotted David lying a few feet away from me. Dodging from bookshelf to bookshelf, I leapt toward him. Up close, I could tell that he was still breathing, and relief filled me, though he appeared to be very weak. The glowing ropes still bound him, and I wasn't sure how to break them, but I knew that it would probably have to be done through magic.

You have unlocked the power of True Sight, Lao Lao reminded me. *Narrow your line of vision and focus your power.*

I obeyed and was stunned when heat traveled out of my eyes like laser beams. The lasers seared away David's ropes, melting them as easily as if they were made of cheese. As soon as I finished, a rush of dizziness swept over me. Using the True Sight had drained me of almost all my energy. But I couldn't stop now. I still had to defeat the Gloomy One.

David stirred and opened his eyes. It was a miracle that his glasses were still in place and undamaged. Before I could shush him, he croaked, "W-Winnie?"

"Aha! There you are!" The Gloomy One turned at the sound and lumbered toward me. Electricity crackled all down the length of his body, from the center of his chest out toward the tips of his fingers.

Crap.

David, who seemed to be wide awake now, yelled, "What the heck is up with your *eyes*—"

"Can you stand?" I demanded.

"I—I think so?"

Too many things were happening at once: David struggling to stand, the Gloomy One's fast-approaching footsteps shaking the whole building, Lao Lao shouting instructions in my head.

You feel drained, but that's just your mind telling you that you're exhausted. You're stronger than that. Push through. Channel my power. Now, more than ever, I regretted that we hadn't had another training session before this battle. Just one would have made a difference. Learning how to refine my magic on the fly was the most stressful thing I'd ever done, including back-to-back piano tests.

Doing my best to focus on only the task at hand, I shoved a mooncake into each of David's hands. "We're going to battle this beast, or die trying," I told him.

"G-great!" he squeaked, in a voice that suggested this wasn't great at all.

I bit into one of the mooncakes, and immediately the familiar warmth entered my body.

My grandmother's words echoed in my ear. *Remember your training. Concentrate on happy feelings. Those are the most powerful!*

Concentrating as hard as I could, I focused on channeling my grandmother's spirit. Energy hummed in the air around me and then within me, heating me up from the inside out. Lao Lao and I hadn't ever successfully combined forces before today, and certainly not for this long, but if ever it was going to work, I needed it to be now.

My insides grew hotter, hotter.

What do we do now, Lao Lao?

Let me guide you, little one.

My arms seemed to move of their own accord, though I recognized that it was my grandmother's will. My fingers unfurled, and blue flames leapt at my fingertips, shooting out and forming an impenetrable protective bubble over David and me.

I didn't have time to stop and marvel at what I'd done. I grabbed my last two mooncakes, one in either hand.

David and I stood our ground, shoulder to shoulder, when the Gloomy One reached us. He had to be twenty feet tall now. Each of his muscles was stretched and defined. Electricity pulsed along his body, some of it jumping from his angry eyes.

You and David will need to join forces to capture this spirit, said my grandmother. *You alone cannot accomplish this job.*

"Concentrate on happy feelings, David!" I ordered. "Use your magic to combine with your overspirit. We have to call this evil spirit's True Name and capture him—together."

"H-happy feelings? What are those?" he squeaked.

"This has been fun, shaman, but playtime is over," snarled the spirit. "Now it's time to *die!*"

Bolts of electricity shot from the Gloomy One's fingers. David and I ducked to either side, and the light hit the ground where we'd both stood just moments ago, burning a black spot into the floor.

It was hard, if not impossible, trying to maintain any happy feelings at the moment. But I knew I had to, if I were to continue channeling Lao Lao's powers and stand a chance against this beast. Before I could summon any pleasant memories, the Gloomy One was upon me.

I opened my mouth to scream. And then I heard him speak in his loud, horrible voice. "Give in, little shamans."

"N-never!" I shouted back. Or at least, I tried to shout, but my voice came out trembly and weak. I was losing my strength, fast.

"You know you can't overpower me. Give in now, and you'll be happier than you were before. You'll see. Being possessed is like an escape from the troubles of your life. Now, doesn't that sound nice?"

"N . . ." I wanted to say no, but this time I couldn't even form the whole word. And now that I thought about it, wasn't there some logic to the spirit's argument? Had I *really* been that happy, while trying to make everyone else around me happy?

"Your whole town will see how much more useful you are when you're at my beck and call. When you're all under my control."

The Gloomy One's words made . . . sense. They made a lot of sense. In fact, I couldn't recall a time in my life when I *hadn't* wanted to be at the spirit's beck and call. Being possessed could only be an improvement to my life.

But then a second voice broke through the haze.

Winnie, are you still there? I'm losing our connection. Can you hear me? Concentrate on happy feelings! No matter what, don't let this spirit fool you. You're stronger than him. You're stronger than you know you are. Concentrate and summon your magic—and mine!

That voice. It was so annoying. Why couldn't it go away?

All I wanted now was to stop fighting. Wouldn't somebody give me a break? Let me rest? They were always demanding I do something more, more, more—Mama, Baba, and Lao Lao.

Wait.

Lao Lao.

It was my grandmother's voice, trying to bring me back to the present. Calling me toward her, away from the grasp of the evil spirit. I'd almost fallen for his dirty tricks. That made me angry—and determined.

With a rush of realization, I obeyed Lao Lao's words and focused on summoning any happy memories.

So I thought of cooking. Of baking red bean brownies with Mama. Of how I always felt after eating a yummy dessert, all warm and fuzzy inside. Channeling all those happy emotions to the forefront of my mind, I threw the two mooncakes at the Gloomy One as hard as I could, just as David did the same.

David and I were on the same wavelength. Blue fire had erupted around him as well, and his eyes were glowing bright red. They looked terrifying, but I knew mine looked the same. Finally, we'd *both* unlocked True Sight.

I turned toward the Gloomy One. And there, at last, was his True Name, written on his forehead in glowing characters.

Hou Yi.

The legendary archer who'd shot down nine suns. Of

course it made sense that Hou Yi's power as a spirit would be taking away sunlight, along with any other source of light around us. If we didn't hurry and defeat him, he would take away our light—*forever.*

Though I'd had my suspicions, I still found it hard to believe. Hou Yi the legend was real, and *he* was the one who'd put this curse on Groton—all to get the essence of the moon. I knew he'd been madly in love with Chang E, but she'd flown to the moon and left him behind. His wanting to take the essence of the moon probably had something to do with that.

If David was shocked, he hid it well. We put our hands on the cookbook and chanted together the words Lao Lao and Joe had taught us for the Naming.

"Evil spirit, no longer will you roam freely in this world. By the powers vested in me, I call you by your True Name and command you to return to your story. I name you— Hou Yi!"

The resulting explosion, I swear, was probably felt around the world. Light burst throughout the bookstore, sending books flying everywhere. The cookbook flew out of David's and my hands, flipping open to the page about the Mid-Autumn Festival, where Hou Yi's story was written.

I covered my eyes to protect them from the light and watched through my fingers as the hulking spirit writhed and twisted. He let out a ferocious roar and grew brighter, forcing me to turn away entirely.

"Y-you haven't won, shamans!" shouted the class three spirit. His deep, booming voice now sounded much higher—and frightened. "This isn't the end. I am only the first of many spirits coming to take over your world. Do you hear me? This is only the beginning—ahhhhh!" The voice was abruptly cut off by a scream, and then, with another burst of light, the spirit disappeared entirely.

For a moment, I couldn't see through all the light, but finally it dimmed.

The last thing I saw was Lao Lao floating beside me. My body felt utterly drained, and my knees crumpled beneath me. Then the world around me burst into a white nothingness. Something heavy hit me on the head, and all turned black.

CHAPTER TWENTY-FOUR

When I came to, I registered the sound of frantic shouting. "Lao . . . Lao?" I murmured.

But it wasn't my grandmother. She was gone, I remembered as the details slowly returned to me. She'd taken the evil spirit back with her to the spirit world.

Beside me, David stirred feebly. "Wus goin' on?" he mumbled. "Are we dead? Am I in heaven?"

There were more shouting voices around me. Then a bunch of the town's police officers stormed into the wreckage of the bookstore.

"They're here, Chief," shouted one officer as he spotted us. "I've found the missing children!"

Dimly, I registered what was going on, and the memories of what had happened earlier rushed back to me. Nearby, the frightened bookstore customers, including Jessamyn, stood huddled with Mr. Stevens. They were no longer frozen, which was a relief. They were covered in dirt from head to foot, and all looked like they'd taken a tumble.

I was no longer in the Department of Supernatural Record-Keeping. Somehow, after banishing the Gloomy

One back to the spirit realm, David and I had ended up on the first floor of the Suntreader.

The overhead lights were working again, so I guessed that the defeat of the evil spirit had restored all of the city's light.

"How are we supposed to explain this to the authorities?" David muttered under his breath.

"Um, well, for starters, we aren't going to tell them the truth." I tried to imagine telling the police that the evil spirit of a legendary figure from Chinese mythology had tried to take all the light in this town for himself, and that we'd defeated him by clobbering him with mooncakes and a magical cookbook. Yeah, that would go over *super* well. Not.

David snorted. "Of course we aren't telling them the truth. But what story should we—?"

"Shhhh. Listen." I raised a finger to my lips and pointed in the direction of the recently unfrozen customers. They were giving the authorities their version of the story, and I could barely hear their voices from where I was sitting. While they spoke, a young officer jotted down notes on her pad.

". . . huge, buff guy with tattoos who looked like he was in a motorcycle gang or something came into this bookstore and started messing everything up," said Mr. Stevens in a shaky voice.

"Those kids chased him out," added the older woman, throwing us a teary, grateful look. She pointed right at me. I jolted. The police officers turned their curious gazes toward

David and me. Not knowing what else to do, I gave a sheepish smile and waved.

Jessamyn piped up. "Then there was this huge explosion. It made all the power in the building go out."

"Yes, we had a citywide power outage just now," said one of the officers. "It was only a matter of time, given all the bad weather we've had lately."

David and I exchanged a meaningful look. Nobody except us knew the true source of the power outage: the Gloomy One draining the whole city of its energy and light.

"So," said the note-taking officer, glancing down at her pad and then up at us again, "that's the full story, then?"

We all nodded. I did my best to look like I wasn't hiding a ginormous secret. Like the fact that the full story included evil spirits on the loose and shamanism.

"Where's the criminal?" she asked. "He must still be somewhere, buried under the wreckage."

"We checked this whole area," said another officer. He shook his head, a mystified expression on his face. "There's no man in sight. It's like he just disappeared."

"He can't have disappeared," she snapped, crossing her arms over her chest. "Search again. Meanwhile, we'll get these children home. If you'll follow me, kids, we'll put you into some cars, and then you'll be on your way home. Your folks have been very worried, and I'm sure they'll be glad to know you're safe and sound."

"H-how late is it?" I asked, suddenly nervous and sure that I didn't want to hear the answer.

One of the officers checked his wristwatch. "It's almost six p.m."

I gulped. Mama was definitely home by now, and Baba would be soon, if he wasn't working overtime tonight. I was in huge trouble, and so was Lisa for letting me leave the house.

We rushed to the police cars parked outside. I'd never been inside a police car, and though I'd found the idea cool before—well, cool as long as it didn't mean I was getting arrested—now I was having trouble finding anything cool or interesting about it. Dread had balled in the pit of my stomach at the thought of facing my family when I got home. There was no way I'd be able to explain the situation to them, and the sight of me arriving in a police car would probably earn me a lecture from Mama.

Yeah, maybe I'd saved the whole city—but at what price?

The police officers divided our groups so that there were two people per car, based on who lived closest to each other. David got to go in his own car, whereas I got stuck with Jessamyn. I protested that I could just bike home, but the officer insisted and placed my bicycle in the trunk.

"Buckle up, kids. I'll get you both home in a jiffy," said one of the officers. "I'm Officer Shapiro. Now, where do you both live?"

After we gave him our addresses, an awkward silence descended upon the car. I tried to ignore the tension by staring out the window as we drove past sprawling lawns and big suburban houses. Even though I'd saved Jessamyn just now, I hadn't forgotten the way she and her friends had been making fun of me since the first day of school. And I wasn't in the mood—nor did I even have the energy—to strike up a polite conversation.

Jessamyn seemed to feel the same way, because she didn't say a single word to me or to Officer Shapiro until we arrived at my house.

"Thank you, Officer," I said as I got out of the car.

"You're welcome," said Officer Shapiro. He took my bike out of the trunk and then gestured for me to lead the way up the driveway.

"Wait!"

I turned around in surprise to find that Jessamyn was leaning her head out the window.

"I—I just wanted to say . . . thank you, Winnie."

I blinked. Okay, so it wasn't as elaborate a thank-you as I deserved, and she still hadn't apologized, but this was more than I'd expected from Jessamyn. I was pretty sure this was the first time Jessamyn had thanked anyone for anything in her whole life.

Smiling slightly, I said, "You're welcome."

"This doesn't mean we're friends," Jessamyn said quickly.

I resisted the urge to roll my eyes. Some things would never change. But that was fine by me. I was beginning to realize that while I might never be friends with the popular kids, I already had some cool people in my corner. Oh, and David, too, I guess.

"See you in school, Jessamyn."

"See you."

Shaking my head, I walked to the door, with Officer Shapiro beside me. The good mood that had flared inside me briefly at hearing Jessamyn's unexpected thank-you quickly dissolved when I realized that I was facing perhaps my greatest obstacle yet: the Mom-inator.

And this time, nobody—not my grandmother's spirit or the police—could save me from her wrath.

As this thought hit me, I considered making a run for it. Too late. Before the police officer even knocked on the door, Mama flung it open, as though she'd been standing behind it, waiting for me all this time. Come to think of it, she probably had.

My mother's eyes were red and puffy, as though she'd been crying. They widened with shock when she saw me standing next to a police officer.

Inwardly I groaned. I could practically hear the thoughts running through my mother's mind at the sight of law enforcement on our doorstep. She probably thought I'd gotten into some serious trouble. In fact, I was surprised she hadn't already fainted.

"Oh—um—hello!" Mama said, clearly uncomfortable with Officer Shapiro's presence.

"Ma'am, your daughter Winnie is a hero," said Officer Shapiro kindly. "I wanted to see to it that she returned home safely. A few of her classmates were in trouble earlier today, but Winnie rushed to save them."

"In trouble?" Mama's jaw dropped in shock. I'd always thought that was an exaggeration that only happened in comics, but my mother was so stunned that her jaw *actually* appeared to have unhinged itself. "What? How?"

"We're working out the details, but I expect the official report will be released to the news tomorrow morning, if not tonight," said the man grimly.

But Mama appeared not to have heard him. Her eyes were fixed on me, and I tried to smile, though I probably looked like I had a toothache instead. "And Winnie *saved* them?"

"She did. I'll let her tell you the whole story herself. Well, if that's all—good evening." Tipping his hat to us, Officer Shapiro turned on his heel and walked smartly down the path toward his car.

When he was gone, I faced Mama. She gaped at me as though she was truly seeing me for the first time. I squirmed, not sure where to begin. "Um . . ."

"Winnie, I—" Mama began. Then she closed her eyes and, after a few drawn-out moments, opened them again. I was startled to see they were filled with tears. "I'm glad you're all right. Do you know how worried we all were?"

"Sorry," I mumbled.

Mama sighed. "It's okay. What matters is that you're safe."

I blinked, surprised. This scenario was turning out way better than any I'd imagined.

"And I hope you didn't forget it's the Mid-Autumn Festival," Mama said.

"Oh yeah, you're right." In the chaos of the day, I'd forgotten. Oh no. I couldn't believe I'd worried my family on the Mid-Autumn Festival, of all days. "Do we have moon-cakes?"

"Yes, but only for dessert," my mother said with a stern expression. "We're eating roast duck and mixed vegetables. I've made pulled noodles, too."

My stomach growled in response to the thought of roast duck. I realized for the first time that I hadn't eaten lunch, and breakfast felt like a bazillion years ago.

Lisa and Baba were both seated at the kitchen table when we entered. My sister was completely unfrozen again, and the sight filled me with relief. Both of them seemed to have heard the whole conversation. They, too, gawked at me in shock. Nothing as interesting as me saving my class-mates had ever happened in the Zeng household.

As Mama piled food onto my plate, I resigned myself to telling the whole story—or, rather, the *nonmagical* version of the story—to my wide-eyed family. When I was done, there was a stunned silence. Everyone stared at me, and I stared at my roast duck as though expecting it to start tap-dancing on my plate.

"Well, aren't you guys going to say anything?" I asked after a while. "It's fine. I'm ready for my punishment." I closed my eyes and held my breath.

"Punishment?" Baba said, his voice full of confusion.

I peeled open one eyelid, then the other. "Yeah, punish-ment. For sneaking out of the house when I was supposed to be studying and playing piano." I figured I'd be in a whole host of trouble at home, despite having saved the world.

Figured it was something that came with the job description. Maybe they'd start talking about how David never skipped piano practice to rescue people or something.

"Oh, and please don't punish Lisa," I added, casting a look at my older sister. Lisa stared at me like I'd sprouted a third hand. "I made her let me sneak out of the house."

"Yeah, she did," Lisa piped up. "I had no part in this."

Okay, so even if it was true, she didn't have to agree with me *that* eagerly. Plus, even if she didn't remember it, I'd just saved her from being frozen forever. My sister owed me her *life*. She should've been showering me with praise.

"We aren't going to punish you, Winnie," said Mama.

I almost dropped my chopsticks in shock. "You aren't?"

"Of course not. It's just as that man said—you're a *hero*. And, well, Baba and I have been talking, and . . . we agreed that perhaps we've been too hard on you both lately. And we're sorry." A sheepish expression crossed Mama's face.

Lisa and I exchanged dumbfounded looks. Our parents were acknowledging that they were hard on us. More than that, they were *apologizing* to us. Put that on the list of Top Ten Anime Plot Twists.

"We're just glad you're both safe and sound," Baba said quietly. "That was a very scary call we got from your school earlier, Winnie, reporting that you'd run off and gone missing."

Guilt shot through me. Tomorrow I'd have to handle my teachers at school, who no doubt had panicked when I bolted straight out of the nurse's office.

"No punishment? Seriously?" Lisa finally spoke up, shooting our parents an incredulous look.

"No punishment," said Mama. She raised an eyebrow. "Unless you both *want* a punishment?"

"No thanks," Lisa said quickly.

"Yeah, I'm good," I added.

Mama smiled. "Let's just enjoy this delicious food."

Lisa and I looked at each other in astonishment and then shrugged. Together, as a family, for the first time in a while, we ate our dinner and caught up with one another.

For dessert, we finished off the meal with Mama's homemade mooncakes. They were delicious, filling, and nonmagical—just the way I liked them.

CHAPTER TWENTY-FIVE

"Okay, you won our bet. I'll do your Chinese homework for a whole month."

That was the single most painful sentence I'd ever uttered out loud. But after the results had come in for the sixth-grade bake sale competition, there was no getting around it: I'd lost my bet with David.

Mrs. Payton's class had raised a total of five hundred twenty-five dollars, and Mr. Burnside's homeroom a whopping six hundred and nine. The results had been pretty close. But that only made it *more* painful to stomach, knowing the other class had beaten mine by such a narrow margin.

Now we were at lunch, and David wouldn't stop gloating at our cafeteria table. He gave a smug grin, which I longed to wipe off his face. "Your class put up a good fight, but mine won in the end—like I knew we would."

"Oh, shut it, Zuo."

"But it's okay. You don't have to do my Chinese homework."

I startled. "I don't?"

David shook his head. "Nah. In fact, I'd rather you *don't* do my work, since I'll only know it's accurate if *I* do it."

"Hey, my Chinese is pretty good, too!" I protested.

"Keep telling yourself that, if it makes you feel better." David stuck his tongue out at me. But I didn't even retaliate. I just stared in surprise. It wasn't like him to not want his prize for winning a bet.

"How come you don't want me to do your work? Did the Gloomy One hit you over the head yesterday or something?" I motioned toward my own forehead.

"Shhhhh! Don't talk about anything . . . *weird* here. People can hear you! They're paying extra attention to us today," David hissed, casting a suspicious glance around the cafeteria.

"Oh, it's not like they'll know what we're talking about anyway."

David and I were sitting at lunch together. His parents had made him some kind of fancy salad that he said resembled the ones he used to get at Stuyvale, but I thought it resembled something Jade would eat.

Meanwhile, I'd packed my *Sailor Moon* lunch box with leftover roast duck and a small mooncake. Jessamyn, Tracy, and Kim passed our table but didn't have any rude comments about my lunch. Actually, they didn't have much to say at all. They scurried past after giving David and me a nod. I guess Jessamyn had talked to the other girls, and that nod was their way of thanking us for rescuing Jessamyn yesterday. The least they could've done was bake us some thank-you brownies, but whatever.

The students and faculty were watching us extra closely today. I'd felt their eyes on us and heard their whispers all day long.

After the local news had reported the mysterious explosion at the Suntreader this morning—noting that the criminal was still at large—we'd basically become famous in this school. People kept coming up to me, asking what it was like to almost die, and really sensitive stuff like that.

I couldn't wait for everything to die down. This was definitely not the kind of popularity I'd wanted in middle school.

"Well, I mean, I figured we're even," David mumbled, speaking so quickly that his words blended together, "since you did kind of save my life yesterday and everything."

Midbite, I grinned. "What was that? I didn't quite hear it."

"I said, chew with your mouth closed, you doofus."

"That is so *not* what you just said!"

Even though on the surface it might not have looked like much had changed between David and me, I got the sense that something had. At least, I respected him more than before. After all, there are some experiences in life that you can't come out of without liking each other, and defeating an evil spirit with the power of mooncakes is one of them.

"I'm kind of screwed, though," I confessed. "I was supposed to finish working on my English presentation yesterday, and obviously that didn't happen. And it's due tomorrow." Yeah, I'd saved Groton and all that, but at the cost of breaking my streak of good grades. Mama and Baba might have decided not to punish me for sneaking out, but I wasn't so sure that mercy would extend to bad grades.

"Well, you can work on the presentation today, can't you?" David pointed out.

"Nope. Gotta study for the pre-algebra test."

David tilted his head to one side and squinted at me.

"What? Is there something on my face?"

"Why don't you just partner up with me? I've got most of the research done, but it's all stuff that we both know anyway, from Chinese school and, well, you know." He did some weird blinking thing with his eye that made me concerned he was having a seizure. Then I realized the truth: he was trying to wink.

"Not following you."

David sighed and rolled his eyes, like he couldn't believe how obtuse I was being. "My presentation topic is the legend of Chang E and Hou Yi."

"Ohhhhh. Hey, you're taking the easy way out!" I accused. "That legend is pretty much all we've been learning about in Chinese school. And we, you know"—I lowered my voice, in case anyone was eavesdropping—"we also kicked Hou Yi's butt."

"That's why I'm being smart about my schoolwork and doing my presentation on what I already know," David said with a shrug and a smug grin. "You're just annoyed you didn't decide to do it in the first place."

I gritted my teeth but had no retort. He was right.

"Anyway, whaddya say?"

I pretended to think about it, but only for a few seconds. "Yeah, I suppose we can team up."

"Don't act like you're doing *me* the favor, Zeng."

"I am, though. Your presentation is going to be a million times better with me as part of it. You'll see."

That night, I invited David over so we could work on the project. He'd already put most of it together, though now that we'd met Hou Yi, it was hard reconciling the gentle Hou Yi from the legends with the mean-spirited jerk he was now. We focused on figuring out who was going to say what for the presentation.

The next day during English class, David and I got up there and taught the whole class about the legend of Chang E and Hou Yi, and we told them a bit about the Mid-Autumn Festival, too. It was too bad we couldn't tell our classmates the truth—that without his love, Hou Yi had become kind of a jerk in the afterlife and had almost ruined our whole town just to get his hands on the essence of the moon.

Our presentation went five minutes over the thirty-minute time limit, but Mrs. Lee didn't seem to care. She said she was so fascinated by the subject that she didn't dock any points for the extra five minutes. We both got A-pluses.

David and I turned to each other and high-fived. And then, at the same moment, we realized that we had just *high-fived*. Like we were *friends*.

Quickly, I turned away and rubbed my hand on the back of my jeans to rid it of any David germs.

"The Chinese midterm is coming up in a few weeks," David said after class was over. We headed out into the packed hallway. "I'm totally going to get the best score."

"Are you kidding me? *I'm* getting the top score."

"Ha! I guess we'll just have to find out."

I crossed my arms over my chest. "Yeah, we will."

And with that, we both turned and marched off in opposite directions.

But nobody, not even David, could ruin my good mood for the rest of the week. By Friday, I'd finished my English presentation *and* my pre-algebra test, and I had a rare, blissfully free weekend. When I got home from school that afternoon, the first thing I did was feed Jade. Then, making sure Lisa was too busy on the phone upstairs to hear me, I bent over and spoke to the rabbit.

"Lao Lao? Are you there?"

Jade stared at me with her huge rabbit eyes for one, two, three Mississippis. I was just considering picking her up and giving her a good shake to see if that might do something when that familiar silvery-white substance rose out of her body. My grandmother's spirit hovered above Jade.

"Lao Lao!"

My grandmother beamed at me, and my chest swelled in happiness. "Winnie. You were magnificent, defeating the spirit of Hou Yi. And I'm happy to report that I've just gotten back from the spirit realm, where he's been locked up in jail."

"There's a jail in the spirit realm?" I said, surprised.

"Of course. Where do you think we keep the bad spirits, like Hou Yi or tax evaders?" Lao Lao chuckled, shaking her head. "Silly girl. The spirits that are prone to chaos are confined in this place and watched over by guards. Unfortunately, though, sometimes breakouts can happen—typically when the awakening of a powerful new shaman causes disruptions in the spirit realm." She raised an eyebrow at me, and I realized that she meant *me*. I was the new shaman who'd caused a disruption in the spirit realm.

"Oh. Oops." I guess the unleashing of the Gloomy One onto Groton had been my fault, even though I'd had no idea what I'd done.

"I also came back to the human realm with an urgent message for you." Lao Lao's expression turned serious. "The Spirit Council believes that the doors to the spirit realm have been damaged beyond repair, at least for the time being. The breach of the Department of Supernatural Record-Keeping is serious. They fear more spirits will be able to find their way out of their stories to the human realm as long as those pathways remain unsealed." My grandmother fixed me with a pressing look. "They want to meet you and make it official that you're a member of the Shaman Task Force, working under the Spirit Council to protect the human world. You'll even get a special badge," she said brightly.

"The Spirit Council wants to *meet* me?" I gaped. "How?"

My grandmother grinned. "You'll have to travel up to the eight hundred and eighty-eighth floor of the Suntreader. We'll go tomorrow, when the headquarters will be open again at ten seventeen a.m."

That was a really random time, but I'd learned by now that there was no use arguing with Lao Lao about the logistics of the spirit realm. It seemed they really didn't abide by the rules of the human world.

I was ready. More ready than I thought I could ever be. Now that I'd unlocked True Sight, I knew I wasn't a fraud, that I could actually *do* this. Join the Shaman Task Force. Save the world.

"I'm ready," I said aloud.

"No, you aren't. There's no way you can greet the Spirit Council wearing those clothes," said my grandmother.

I groaned. "Lao Lao, you don't have to tell me. I already know that." It wasn't like I planned to greet the all-important Spirit Council with the math camp T-shirt and sweatpants I was currently wearing. Even *I* knew that wasn't proper. "I just mean—now that I've unlocked True Sight, I feel ready."

"True Sight isn't a power that you can always access once you've unlocked it," explained my grandmother.

"You'll have to work at it each time you're in battle. But you're definitely closer to mastering it than you were weeks ago." She cracked a grin. "Now, let's go do something nice in the meantime. Get you freshened up. Maybe bake some mooncakes."

I shot her an alarmed look. "M-mooncakes?"

"I'm just kidding. Maybe something less dangerous," my grandmother said with a wink, and I laughed.

Whatever baked treat we decided on, with Lao Lao by my side, it would turn out absolutely delicious.

RECIPES FROM WINNIE ZENG'S COOKBOOK

One of the best gifts my grandmother passed down to me is her love of food. Now, reader, I'm passing a couple of my favorite recipes on to you! They're Winnie Zeng's specialties—and everyone, even Lisa, has to admit I have a knack for making mooncakes and red bean brownies. These treats can be eaten around specific holidays, like mooncakes for the Mid-Autumn Festival, or whenever you're craving something sweet. Just be careful not to accidentally unleash any spirits—good or evil—when you're baking them!

Before you start baking, be sure to ask for an adult's permission and help.

Happy baking!
—Winnie

Lao Lao's Mooncakes

(Makes 12 cakes)

Ingredients:

2 tablespoons vegetable oil

$1/4$ cup golden syrup or honey

$1/2$ teaspoon alkaline water

$1/2$ cup cake flour

$1/2$ cup all-purpose flour

2 cups red bean paste

1 miniature mooncake mold

1 egg

1 tablespoon water

Optional: 1 packet essence of the moon

Directions:

In a mixing bowl, whisk together the vegetable oil, golden syrup (or honey), and alkaline water until the mixture is blended. Use a wooden spoon to stir in the cake flour and the all-purpose flour. Gently knead the mixture until it comes together, taking care not to overwork the dough. Wrap the dough with plastic wrap and let it sit for 45 minutes.

Preheat your oven to 350°F. Split the red bean paste filling into 12 equal pieces. Using your hands, roll each piece into a ball about the size of a golf ball, or about $1 3/4$ inches in diameter.

To form each mooncake, scoop out 1 tablespoon of dough. Use a rolling pin to roll out the dough between two pieces of parchment paper until it's about $3^1/_2$ to 4 inches in diameter. Place a ball of red bean paste filling in the center of the dough, and wrap the dough around the paste. Gently press and squeeze the dough in your palm until it completely covers the filling.

Set the mooncake mold on a countertop or another hard surface. Place the dough ball in your mooncake mold and push the plunger down until there is resistance; then lift the mooncake mold up, pushing out the mooncake with the plunger. Place the mooncake on a parchment-lined baking sheet. Repeat the process until you have used all the dough.

Bake the mooncakes at 350°F for 6 to 8 minutes. While you wait, whisk an egg with a dash of water in a small mixing bowl.

Once the mooncakes are done baking, remove them from the oven and let them cool for 10 minutes. Brush the egg wash onto the cooled mooncakes. Return them to the oven for another 7 to 10 minutes, or until the tops are golden brown.

Take the mooncakes out of the oven and let them cool completely. For optimal enjoyment, store the mooncakes in an airtight container for up to 48 hours. But if you, like Winnie, would rather eat them fresh, go for it!

Mama's Red Bean Brownies
(Makes 1 batch)

Ingredients:
2 cups dry red beans, soaked and cooked, or 1 package
   (500 grams) red bean paste

$1/_2$ cup maple syrup

$1/_2$ cup coconut oil

1 teaspoon vanilla extract

4 eggs

$1/_2$ cup cacao powder

$1/_2$ cup semisweet chocolate chips

Optional: 2 tablespoons powdered sugar

Directions:
Preheat your oven to 350°F. Lightly grease a baking dish with coconut oil.

In a mixing bowl, beat the cooked red beans or red bean paste together with the maple syrup, coconut oil, and vanilla extract. Mix in the eggs, cacao powder, and chocolate chips.

Transfer the red bean brownie mixture to the baking dish, and bake in the oven for 30 to 40 minutes, or until a toothpick inserted in the center comes out clean.

Let the red bean brownies cool. Dust the top with powdered sugar if desired, and enjoy with friends and family (or on your own—though be careful not to eat them all at once!).

ACKNOWLEDGMENTS

It is surreal that this is the fifth time I'm writing acknowledgments, for what is my fifth published novel. When the idea for the Winnie Zeng series came to me back in 2018, I had no idea that one day a whole team of publishing professionals at Penguin Random House would so love this story of a Chinese American girl trying to navigate middle school and save the world. And now it's my honor that young readers are meeting Winnie Zeng. I'm utterly blessed to have the opportunity to write Winnie's adventures and to have so many wonderful people in my corner cheering me on.

As always, thank you first and foremost to Penny Moore, my amazing agent, who was the first publishing professional to ever tell me yes—and who has said yes to me many times since. Thank you, Penny, for giving me the writing career of my dreams. Thank you for giving young Asian readers the stories they deserve, in which they see themselves as full-fledged, powerful heroes. Every book on your list is one that I desperately wish I'd had many years ago—and that I'm so thankful that readers have now. We are changing this corner of our world, and there is no one else I'd rather be on this wild publishing journey with.

Thank you to Tricia Lin, my whip-smart and enthusiastic editor. Tricia, you were the first editor to ask for a call when the Winnie Zeng series was on submission to publishers. Even before the call was finished, I knew you were the one. You understood the heart of this series from the get-go. What else is there to say? I thought that being published was my greatest dream, but having a brilliant Chinese American editor for my Chinese American series is truly the highest privilege, an honor I never dared to hope for. I'm deeply moved by how you've championed the Winnie Zeng series and pushed me to make this book better than I could have on my own. Because of you, Winnie's magical story will reach many young readers. Xiè xie. Thank you.

Thank you to my hardworking publishing team at Penguin Random House: Caroline Abbey, Michelle Nagler, Mallory Loehr, Sylvia Bi, Andrea Lau, April Ward, Janet Foley, Rebecca Vitkus, Barbara Bakowski, Alison Kolani, Nathan Kinney, Catherine O'Mara, Sophia Cohen Smith, Emma Benshoff, Elizabeth Ward, John Adamo, Kris Kam, Joey Ho, and Dominique Cimina. Thank you to my brilliant cover illustrator, Sher Rill Ng. Thank you all so much for being endlessly enthusiastic about the Winnie Zeng series from the start and for making this book possible. I am so grateful for your support.

Thank you to the book-blogging community for being

there with me from the launch of my debut to this book, my fifth. Authors owe you all so much, and I can't adequately say how much I appreciate your love for our books. Thank you for talking about them and helping them reach readers.

Last, but certainly not least, to my family and friends: Thank you for being by my side through the many ups and downs of my publishing journey. I am the luckiest author to get to embark on this writing adventure with the best people in my corner. I can't wait to keep sharing my stories with you.